"Good night, Bliss. Go inside now."

Something that looked like disappointment crossed her face, then quickly disappeared. She nodded and turned. Bob watched Bliss disappear inside, watched the door close and the light go on.

With nothing left to do but leave, Bob trudged down the steps toward his truck. "What's wrong with you?" he whispered. "You told her to go inside. What did you expect?"

"Bobby, wait."

Bob looked over his shoulder to see Bliss in the doorway. "What?"

"Come here."

"Why?"

She affected an exasperated look. "I may live downtown, but I do have neighbors. Do you want me to give them something to talk about, or are you going to come over here?"

Bob chuckled despite himself. What in the world was this woman up to?

KATHLEEN Y'BARBO is a tenth-generation Texan and mother of three grown sons and a teenage daughter. She is a graduate of Texas A&M University and an award-winning novelist of Christian and young-adult fiction. Kathleen is a former treasurer for American Christian Fiction Writers and is a member of Inspirational Writers Alive, Words for the Journey, and The Authors Guild. Find out more about Kathleen at www.kathleenybarbo.com.

Books by Kathleen Y'Barbo

HEARTSONG PRESENTS

Don't miss out on any of our super romances. Write to us at the following address for information on our newest releases and club information.

Heartsong Presents Readers' Service
PO Box 721
Uhrichsville, OH 44683

Or visit www.heartsongpresents.com

Wedded Bliss

Kathleen Y'Barbo

Heartsong Presents

To Linda Kozar and Danelle Woody, precious sisters in Christ.

A note from the Author:
I love to hear from my readers! You may correspond with me by writing:

Kathleen Y'Barbo
Author Relations
PO Box 721
Uhrichsville, OH 44683

ISBN 978-1-59789-616-0

WEDDED BLISS

Our mission is to publish and distribute inspirational products offering exceptional value and biblical encouragement to the masses.

PRINTED IN THE U.S.A.

one

Latagnier, Louisiana

Today success smelled like fresh paint and coffee grounds. If all went well, Monday morning it would smell like buttercream frosting, pecan pralines, and freshly baked wedding cakes.

Bliss Denison held the open package of dark-roasted chicory blend and inhaled its familiar aroma one more time before dumping two rounded tablespoons into the old-fashioned percolator. "There's nothing better than a hot cup of coffee on a chilly February day, especially in an old place like this."

Even now as she traced a stencil pattern on the brick wall, Bliss could barely believe she stood in a homey but ancient building in her tiny hometown of Latagnier rather than performing her usual Friday morning duties of presiding over the gleaming kitchens of Austin's exclusive Bentley Crown Hotel.

Who would have thought a routine drive home from work on an icy Tuesday evening in November would have changed not only her career but also her entire life?

"All the way up the ladder only to land right back where I started." She sighed. "Well, next door anyway."

Her first real job, after years of tagging along behind her grandfather at the sawmill, had been next door at the now-defunct Latagnier Pharmacy. Where a wall of windows now pierced red brick and thick white mortar, old Mr. Gallier used to mix compounds by hand and seemingly see through walls to remind a sixteen-year-old Bliss that she was not employed to read the teen magazines but rather to straighten them. Mr. Gallier seemed to know that she hired on as much for the

5

pittance she earned as for the fact that his son, Landon, was also on the payroll.

Bliss's heart lurched at the thought of Landon Gallier. Hair as black as night brushed his shoulders and jutted out of his football helmet to frame a face that remained etched in Bliss's mind even now, silly as that seemed. And oh, that smile. Crooked, with just a hint of mischief, that same smile was used to fool parents into thinking him harmless.

He wasn't, of course, but that was part of his charm—a ruse he couldn't have pulled off without his partner in crime, Bobby Tratelli. Bliss smiled.

The lure of the forbidden, the joy of pulling the wool over their parents' eyes, these were the guilty pleasures of a youth spent in a town where everyone knew everyone else. To get away with anything was an amazing feat, but to know that the town bad boy was held in great esteem by the older generation made his attentions all the more delicious.

Landon called her once at the Bentley in Austin. He left an almost unintelligible message that made Bliss wonder if the man had been intoxicated when he dialed the phone. She should have returned the call. Stubbornness, however, advised her to wait for him to call again when he sobered up. He hadn't. That was more than a decade ago.

Just last year, her mother called to inform her that Landon had taken a job overseas with a company that put out oil well fires. They'd been working to cap an explosion on an offshore rig when Landon fell to his death in the waters beneath the flaming platform.

Mama offered to send a clipping, but Bliss declined. She preferred to remember Landon as the boy upon whom she'd bestowed the honor of her first crush.

The roar of a large brown delivery truck obscured her view of the front window, drawing Bliss from her thoughts. The bridal shop that now filled the space next door was going to be as good for business as the pharmacy would have been for her memories. She watched as the driver carried boxes inside Wedding Belles and decided to pay a visit to the owner.

While the coffee perked, Bliss emptied the single brown sack she'd hauled from the grocer on Martin Street. True to what her physical therapist claimed, the brisk walk had done her good. It would balance out the contraband caffeinated delight now brewing.

The coffeepot gave one last gurgle; then silence—and fresh coffee—reigned. Bliss pushed aside the ancient kitchen stool to retrieve one of her grandmother's Apple Blossom coffee cups.

On impulse, she grabbed another one and set it on the tray along with the sugar bowl, creamer, and two Gorham Chantilly spoons. A handful of pecan pralines completed the tray as she slipped into her shoes and headed next door.

From the street, the building that used to be the pharmacy didn't look much different as a bridal shop except for the contents behind the single broad window. The redbrick facade still sported double wooden doors reached by four wide steps.

Before the accident, she would have climbed them two at a time. Today, however, Bliss grasped the familiar black iron rail and eased up the steps to reach for the brass handle, its gleaming surface polished by four generations of Latagnier's shoppers.

Warm vanilla scent met Bliss as she balanced the tray and pulled the door open with her free hand. In the back of the store, a lanky blond in jeans and a blue sweater rose above the sea of white gowns on a wooden ladder. She swung around at the sound of the front door's jangling bell.

"Welcome to Wedding Belles." The woman gasped and nearly bolted off the ladder. "Bliss Denison? I can't believe it's you!"

Bliss caught the tray just before the contents slid over the edge. "Neecie?" She stepped out of the way of the door and froze. "Neecie Trahan? Last time I saw you, you were playing saxophone in the Latagnier High marching band."

Neecie skittered down the ladder and wove her way through shimmering gowns toward Bliss. "And you were burning cookies in home ec."

Bliss nudged the tray. "Good thing I didn't bring cookies. I never did figure out how to keep the bottoms from turning black."

"Oh, goodness." Neecie gestured toward the back of the store. "Come on and sit down. Are those pralines? Here, let me take that."

She allowed Neecie to take the tray and wondered, for a moment, if sympathy rather than manners had dictated her offer. Relieved of the burden, Bliss easily followed the owner of Wedding Belles to a white iron table set beneath an arbor of climbing roses that almost looked real. "This is beautiful."

"One of my clients was a photographer. I traded her the arbor for an ecru gown with seed pearls and lace overlay." Neecie reached for a white basket brimming with colorful floral cloth and retrieved two napkins, then handed one dotted with tiny red roses to Bliss. "I figured it would make the place look less like a drugstore. Occasionally I even rent the thing out for weddings."

Bliss's gaze swept the room as she eased into the nearest metal chair. "It certainly doesn't look like the place I remember." She wrinkled her nose. "Doesn't smell like it, either. How did you ever get that disinfectant scent out of here?"

"Vanilla candles and elbow grease."

The front door jangled, and a postman walked in. "Your mail slot's stuck again, Neecie." He glanced in Bliss's direction. "Well, I'll be. Is that you, Bliss Denison?"

She nodded while her mind searched for the name of the stranger. "It is."

A moment later, Bliss found herself catching up on old times with the person she used to babysit as a teenager. He'd been a toddler then, barely out of diapers, and now he worked for the post office.

Suddenly, Bliss felt old. Very old.

"Get that fixed, Neecie," he said as he headed for the door. "Good to see you, Bliss," he added. "You don't look nearly as old as I expected."

"Thank you." When the door shut, she added, "I think."

"Let's have that coffee, shall we?" Neecie smoothed the front of her sweater and shook her perfectly coiffed head, revealing sparkling diamond studs in her earlobes. Bliss felt quite drab and underdressed. "So, what brings you back here?"

"I'm your neighbor, actually." Bliss tucked a wayward strand of the mess she'd tried to capture into a ponytail this morning behind her ear and gestured to their common wall. "I bought the Cake Bake."

"Did you, now?" Her smile deepened the lines at her temples. "What're you going to do with it?"

How much to tell her? While Neecie had once been a confidant on whom Bliss could rely, the years had come and gone. The last thing Bliss would tolerate was sympathy. Better to be brief, concise, and casual.

"Monday morning, it reopens." She affected a casual air and sipped at her coffee. "I'm still going to bake cakes, but I'm taking it easy. I plan to be open three days a week—Monday, Wednesday, and Friday—and one Saturday a month." She paused to fumble with her napkin, then met her old friend's gaze. "Everyone's talking about simplifying their lives. I reached a point where it was no longer an option. My life's so simple that I even live above the store."

Bliss held her breath and waited for the reaction. For the inevitable questions.

After all, what sort of sane woman would leave a job like

the one she had in Austin to bake cakes part-time? Who leaves a magnificent loft with a view of the capitol to live in a drafty old building over a cake shop?

Neecie stared for a moment before her smile broadened. "I declare you're brilliant. Good for you. You were in Austin, I heard. Working at the Bentley?" She gave Bliss a sideways glance. "That's a really nice place. I'm impressed."

"So"—Bliss reached for a praline—"what about you? What have you been up to since graduation?"

"The usual story. Got married, had kids. Got unmarried. Now I own this slice of heaven."

Neecie paused to sip at her coffee while Bliss tried not to gawk. Twenty-five years of time apart summed up so succinctly. Could she do that, as well?

Of course, she could. *Went to school, went to work, rammed my car into the Congress Street bridge, bought a cake shop.*

"Bliss, we all left high school with an idea of how things would turn out. I can't say that I expected this, but you know what?"

Bliss dabbed at the corner of her mouth with the napkin. "What's that?"

"Things didn't turn out like I planned." She met Bliss's stare. "But, I'm blessed, hon, and that's all there is to it. So many of our classmates can't say that. I mean, sure, I would have chosen happily ever after with the man of my dreams over single parenting. And I'd prefer shopping till I drop over shop owning, but it is what it is, you know?"

She did.

"Well, I applaud your decision to drop out of the rat race." Neecie reached to pat the top of Bliss's hand. "Wish I'd thought of it. I tried taking Saturdays off. Left a sign on the door saying only to call in case of bridal emergency."

"A bridal emergency?" Bliss shook her head. "Is there such a thing?"

Neecie hooted with laughter. "You'd be amazed at the calls I get. One gal called to say she missed her fitting on Friday because the hogs got out. Said she couldn't come on Monday because they were getting a new batch of chickens."

"Oh no."

"Oh yes." Neecie shrugged. "Now I'm closed Sundays and Mondays. And I don't answer the business line on those days, bridal emergency or not. I get two days off, and the Lord gets a woman who can actually pay attention in church."

Ouch. When had she last managed that feat? For that matter, with Sunday mornings one of the busiest in the hotel, when had she last sat in a church pew? She immediately made a note to go with her mother to next Sunday's later service.

After all, working late nights at the hotel had robbed her of any ability to remember what it was like to be a morning person.

Neecie seemed to understand Bliss's need to refrain from comment. She made small talk about recipes, high school friends, and the latest episode of *Dr. Phil*. Safe topics exhausted, they lapsed into companionable silence.

Only then did Bliss notice the lovely music. Seemingly coming from all around her, the soft acoustic hymn faded and another began.

"I've never heard music like this," Bliss finally said. "It's beautiful."

"My Christmas present. My children love music. My daughter, Hannah, collected the music to every hymn she could find. That's my son Andrew, the high school–aged skateboard designer, playing guitar. Hannah's accompanying him on the harp." Neecie pointed over her head to the corner of the shop. "The surround sound was wired up by the twins, mechanical geniuses Jake and Josh."

Bliss shook her head. "You have four kids?" She gave her friend a searching look. "How did you manage to do that,

Neecie? You look amazing."

Her friend chuckled. "Well, hon, it happened in the usual way, but thanks."

She felt her cheeks grow warm. "Oh, that's not what I meant."

Neecie laughed and popped another praline in her mouth. "Loosen up, Bliss," she said when she'd swallowed. "I know what you meant. I'm just teasing."

The bell jangled as the door opened to reveal a gorgeous but flustered-looking young woman. Her suit jacket hung just awry of center, caught in the pull of the briefcase hanging from her shoulder. She quickly made an adjustment and smoothed her hair. By the time she and Neecie met halfway in a warm embrace, the woman seemed to have found her confidence.

Holding her customer at arm's length, Neecie shook her head. "Amy, honey, what's wrong?"

"Nothing." The woman's formerly poised expression sank. "Everything. Just tell me the dress is ready for a final fitting, because I've got a plane to catch and a contract to negotiate in London, and my wedding planner hasn't returned my call for two days."

Bliss exchanged a look with Neecie, then rose. "I should get back to the shop."

"Thanks so much for the coffee break. We'll catch up more later." Neecie rested her hand on Bliss's shoulder for a second. "I'm so glad we're neighbors again."

"So am I."

Bliss grabbed a daisy-strewn napkin from the basket and stacked the remaining pralines on it. The tray securely in hand, she made her way toward the door.

She got all the way back to the Cake Bake's kitchen before she realized she hadn't thought to ask Neecie how she came to own the old pharmacy. "Guess I'll leave that one for another day."

✌

"Daddy, please listen. I'm about to board the plane, and I won't be able to speak to you again until I get to London. Everything's completely under control. All you have to do is read the wedding planner's weekly report and occasionally check on a few details."

"If everything's under control, Amy, why do the details need checking on?" Bob Tratelli pushed back from the desk and whirled around to face the window.

"The details need checking on because the wedding's only six weeks away," came his daughter's sweet but exasperated reply.

"It is just six weeks, isn't it?" An image of Amy with skinned knees and a gap-toothed smile came to mind. It was quickly replaced by the photograph on the corner of his desk, the engagement photograph of the gorgeous brunette vice president who could handle the controls of an airplane almost as well as her old man.

Where had all the time gone?

"I just e-mailed Esteban's contact information to you. If you don't want to handle it, put Yvonne on the job."

No doubt his secretary would do a fine job of handling the details of Amy's wedding. Everyone knew she practically ran Tratelli Aviation from her desk outside his office suite, and most of the time that suited him just fine. With the paperwork under control, Bob could give his full attention to the hands-on part of running the business his father founded. He glanced at Amy's smiling photo again. Yvonne could do it, but this would be his last act of fatherly love before giving Amy away to another man.

A question occurred. "Who is Esteban?"

Bob couldn't miss the exasperated sigh. "Our wedding coordinator. Remember, you and I met with him back in January at the Excelsior."

"Excelsior? The one in New York or—"

"Baton Rouge, Daddy. Esteban's offices are in Baton Rouge." She paused. "Remember, he was the one with the purple suit."

Bob searched his brain. A vague memory of himself and Amy and a man in a purple suit surrounded by wedding cakes and plates of grilled chicken came to mind—one of several, as his daughter insisted on visiting a half dozen coordinators. But only one insisted on purple from head to toe, even to the streak in his hair.

"Ah, Esteban," he said as the image of a distinctly odd man with a thick accent came to mind. "Wasn't he the one who kept calling me Mr. Fanelli?"

Amy laughed. "That's the one. He comes highly recommended, and he's being paid well to handle everything. All you have to do is look over the weekly reports and make the occasional phone call to see how things are going."

"Can't you do that from London?"

Silence. In the background, he heard a boarding call for London.

"So when's the last time you talked to this Esteban fellow? Should I call him today or let it go for a week or so?"

"Today, Daddy, please. I'm sure he's been busy."

"Busy?" Bob tried to read between the lines of his daughter's cryptic comment. "Does this mean he's not calling you back? You know what I taught you about vendors who don't return phone calls."

"Yes, Daddy, I know, but he's not an aviation vendor. He's a wedding planner. The best in the state. That means he's busy."

"All right, then, you're busy, too. Can't you change your plans and make your honeymoon and these contract negotiations in London coincide? I'm sure your fiancé would understand, and it would give this Esteban fellow a little more time to do whatever it is he does." Bob paused, knowing full well Amy wasn't buying a bit of this. Still, he had to try. "Besides,

England's not half bad this time of year. You could hold off on the flight today and have the preacher marry the two of you this weekend. Say, why don't I make a couple of calls and get you two into a castle somewhere instead of that Greek cruise you wanted to take? I'm sure—"

"Daddy."

Only Amy Tratelli could make a single word speak volumes. "Look, honey," he said slowly, "I know you've worked hard on landing this contract, but can't you handle the rest of the negotiations from Latagnier?"

"You're not serious." Again a boarding call interrupted their conversation. "I've got to go, Daddy. Please just do this."

He watched as the wind sock at the end of runway B lifted and caught a stiff north breeze. "All right, so this is a big deal. Surely there's someone you trust to see to the details." Bob forced a chuckle. "It's not like I'll remove you as vice president if you delegate this one."

"Daddy." A well-placed pause was followed by a sigh. "Stop kidding around."

Bob's heart wrenched. How very much she sounded like her mother. If only Karen were alive. She'd be up to her eyeballs in wedding plans and never complain a moment, even when the plans changed or a pressing business trip intervened.

But Amy was more like him than Karen. The business had become Amy's life. Sometimes her fierce dedication to Tratelli Aviation caused Bob to wonder if she had any more room in her life for the husband she was about to wed.

"If it makes you feel any better," she said, "Chase has taken on a three-week audit here in London. He's due to arrive on Tuesday." Her giggle took him on a quick trip back to her childhood once more. "Why would I want to come home when my fiancé is here?"

"Why indeed?" Bob rubbed at the ache in his temple. "Amy, you don't know what you're asking. The only thing I had to do for my wedding to your mother was show up at the right place wearing the clothes she picked out for me."

"No," she said softly, "but I know *who* I'm asking."

"Three weeks? I'll give you two weeks, Amy," he said. "If you're not home by then, the wedding's off."

"Yeah, right." Amy chuckled. "Just leave it to Yvonne and stop worrying about it, all right?" She paused. "Please?"

Bob lifted his gaze to the brilliant blue sky and swallowed the rest of his objections. He'd handle this. For Amy. And for Karen.

"Sure, honey, whatever you say. I'm sure Yvonne would love to take over the role of wedding planner while you're gone."

"No, Daddy, we've got a wedding planner. Hold on a sec. I've got a beep."

While he waited, Bob hit the pager and called for Yvonne. The pager buzzed three times before his daughter's breathless voice flooded his ear.

"All right. Sorry," Amy said. "Now, do us both a favor and take a deep breath. The wedding will come off without a hitch, and Yvonne will do just fine with the details until I get back. Now I must go. I love you, Daddy. Tell Yvonne thanks for me."

Yvonne. Bob punched the button again. Where was she?

He settled the phone back on its cradle and stared out at the horizon. Likely as not, Yvonne was just down the hall making coffee. Or maybe she'd stepped out to run an errand.

No matter. As Amy said, everything was under control.

Besides, it was a great day for flying. An absence of clouds and a slight breeze tempted him to walk away from the confines of his corner office and take to the brilliant blue skies. Maybe the Cessna. Or possibly that little jet he was thinking of purchasing.

A check of his watch assured Bob he had plenty of time to make the drive to Baton Rouge and be back in time to change for dinner. Dinner. Where was he supposed to be tonight? There were plans of some sort, something vaguely important.

Only his PDA knew for sure.

Well, his PDA and Yvonne.

He punched her line once more. Odd that he got nothing but silence in return.

Snagging his flight jacket, Bob palmed his truck keys and bounded for the door. Whatever awaited him tonight, surely it wouldn't happen before six or seven. He could be back well before then.

As he rounded the corner, he slammed into an empty chair. Yvonne's empty chair.

Taped to the back was an envelope with his name on it. Bob ripped it open and read the note. He sank into the chair and slapped his forehead. How could he have forgotten? Yvonne had penciled in the dates on his desk calendar.

This was awful.

A mess.

And worse, he'd caused the whole thing when he gave his most loyal employee a gift on her twenty-fifth anniversary with the company.

Just to be sure, he read it again. "You were on the phone with Amy, and I didn't want to interrupt to say good-bye. The temp service is sending someone over on Monday. See you in three weeks. Aloha, boss, and thanks again for the vacation!"

two

Two weeks later

"It'll be fine, Daddy," Amy said. "I'll only be gone another week. I'm taking in the sights in London while my darling finishes the audit he's working on."

Bob gripped the phone so hard he expected it to snap at any moment. "Can't you and Chase take in the sights around Latagnier? You've got a wedding in a month."

"A month and two days," his daughter reminded him. "Besides, you've been getting the reports, right? Things ought to be sailing along." When he didn't immediately respond, she added, "You have been getting the reports from the wedding planner, haven't you?"

"Oh," he said casually, "I'm sure they're around here somewhere."

A nervous chuckle rolled toward him from the other side of the line. "Of course, Yvonne wouldn't let something like that slip. Just ask her. I'm sure she has them."

"Well, there's a bit of an issue with asking Yvonne. She's in Hawaii until a week from Monday."

"Hawaii?" Was it his imagination, or had his daughter's voice gone up a full octave?

"Her anniversary bonus, remember? The woman's been with Tratelli Aviation since you were two. I forgot I promised her a vacation this month." He paused and tried to figure out how to convince Amy of what he was about to say. "Everything will be fine. As soon as we hang up, I'm going to ask the temp for the reports."

"Promise?"

"Yes, dear," he said. "I'm buzzing her now."

He hurried to hang up, fully expecting his temp to respond quickly to his page. When she didn't, he tried the intercom.

"Jeanette, I just realized I haven't seen any of the wedding planner's reports. Would you bring them to me? There should be two of them plus any old ones Amy attached to the e-mail."

Bob released the button on the intercom and waited. Two weeks and three temps later, he was wishing he hadn't been so generous with Yvonne.

It was selfish of him to feel that way, and he knew it. Without Yvonne, he'd be a floundering single dad who never learned to braid hair or tie a bow. Rather than feel sorry for himself that he was lost without Yvonne, Bob knew he should be thanking the Lord for providing her. And for causing the dear woman to stick with him all these years, even past the age when most would have taken retirement. Surely without God's intervention, Yvonne would have come to her senses and fled a decade ago.

"Mr. Tarantino?"

"Tratelli," he corrected. "Why don't you just call me Bob?"

"All right, Mr. Bob. What kind of report did you say you wanted? Something on weeding planes?"

He sighed. Yvonne would be back soon. This was doable.

In the meantime, he'd figure a way to communicate with the latest in a line of temps. At least this one hadn't smelled as if she bathed in gardenias, and she certainly wasn't as distracted as the first woman the agency sent. That gal had put a call through to Tokyo, then punched the hold button and forgotten to tell him.

Another sigh, this for the phone bill and the lengthy apology he had to give his Japanese customer. And for the fact that temps were hard to find in a town as tiny as Latagnier.

If Yvonne didn't come back soon, he might have to sink to the ultimate low: calling his mother for help. Amalie Breaux

Tratelli would handle this and anything else that came her way.
She always had.

The thought was tempting, but with Mama soon to turn eighty-six, and Pop still spry at ninety, the last thing he intended to do was haul them back from their annual visit to the Tratelli family home in California. He knew how much Pop loved the brief time he spent there each year, even if his real home now was here in Latagnier. Mama said it made him feel connected to his parents. Bob thought it might be more than that.

Bob knew this yearly visit, always timed to coincide with the Oscars, was his father's way of honoring the parents who encouraged him and loved him. No way would he call them back from such a mission.

Besides, February in California was highly preferable to February in Latagnier, Louisiana. If not for the wedding, he, too, might. . .

"The wedding! What did you ask me? Oh yes, the wedding planner," Bob said slowly. "I think his name is Enrique or Edward or. . ." He paused to think. "No, it's Esteban. Yes, that's it. The contact information should be in Yvonne's inbox. Look under Weddings by Esteban. It's a Baton Rouge number, I think. Or maybe New Orleans."

A long pause. "I don't see anything in the inbox. Just some memos and a flyer for a spring fair at church."

"A flyer?" Bob shook his head and rose. "I think you're looking in the wrong inbox. I'm referring to the inbox on Yvonne's e-mail program."

"E-mail?"

Bob rounded the corner to see his latest temp rifling through Yvonne's desk. "What are you looking for?" He held his hands up as if to fend off another of the woman's silly answers, then glanced up at the clock. "Never mind. Say, why don't you call it a day?"

"Call it a day?" She pushed back from the desk, revealing

a blinding combination of rainbow-striped skirt and brilliant orange blouse. "But it's only twelve thirty. I just got back from lunch."

"I realize that." He cleared his throat. "But I'm feeling generous. Surely you've got other things you could be doing."

"Well. . ." Her smiled broadened. "I do have some laundry I've been putting off."

"Laundry, excellent. Now I suggest you get to it. Oh, and go ahead and take tomorrow off."

He watched the woman gather her things and rise. "Are you sure? I mean, I wouldn't want to leave you here without decent help."

"It's happened before," Bob said casually, "and I've managed. Now, go. Hurry before I change my mind."

"Suit yourself, Mr. Tarantino."

In the fastest move she'd made all day, the woman sprinted for the door. She left in her wake a desk littered with papers, a phone off the hook, and a computer with a suspicious blue screen.

"That's Tratelli. Bob Tratelli." He shrugged as the door swung shut. "Never mind. Funny how the one time you actually heard me say something without repeating it was when I told you to go home."

No matter. Tomorrow was Wednesday. Maybe he'd take the rest of the week off.

"Now, to find those wedding reports." He pushed the chair out of the way and reached for the wad of documents on the floor beneath the desk. "This looks like a good place to start. If I'm lucky, I might not be here all night."

Bob searched for fifteen minutes; then a stroke of brilliance sent him hurrying back to his computer to find the contact information for his daughter's wedding planner. He left two messages with Esteban in the span of an hour, then climbed into his truck. If the wedding planner wouldn't call him, he'd pay a call on the wedding planner.

ॐ

The truck rolled to a stop in front of Esteban's Baton Rouge shop exactly ninety minutes later. Bob threw it into park, then stretched the kinks out of his shoulders.

Amy would owe him for this one. He shook his head. "I could've been flying today. Good thing I love you so much, kiddo," he muttered to himself.

Staring at the elaborately decorated and curtained window with the gold leaf sign that read WEDDINGS BY ESTEBAN, Bob groaned. The last thing he'd ever want to make his living at was planning weddings. Whatever made a person do it on purpose was beyond him, although he knew from experience they made plenty of money at it.

Bob made one last attempt to phone the wedding planner to make an appointment before hanging up and slipping the phone into his shirt pocket. "All right," he said as he strode toward the door, "let's talk weddings, Esteban."

Before he reached the double doors, his eyes registered a padlock and an eviction notice taped to the door. A call to his buddy in the Baton Rouge police department, and Bob learned that the wedding planner had fled Baton Rouge, and there was no hope of him returning to complete the arrangements for Amy's wedding.

At least not from inside the jail cell that awaited him.

He sat back against the soft leather of his truck's seat and closed his eyes. What were the odds that the only wedding he'd ever have to be a part of would involve a man who decided to take his money and run off?

Bob scrubbed at his face with his hands and exhaled. "Now what, Lord? You know I can't disappoint Amy, but I don't have a clue what I'm doing. I never thought I'd pray this, but could You show me how to marry off my daughter?"

He opened his eyes and waited for the Lord to present a plan. While he waited, he ticked off the possibilities in his mind.

Calling Amy might result in unnecessary panic, so he set that alternative aside for now. His mother would fly back immediately and miss attending the Oscars ceremony this weekend, so he couldn't phone her until next week at the earliest.

Then it came to him. Hire another wedding planner. Surely Esteban was not the only wedding planner in town. There had to be someone else in the city who would take on the responsibility of seeing the wedding through to the ceremony.

"Thank You, Lord. That's a brilliant idea."

Bob reached for his laptop and connected it to his phone to pull up the Internet. He'd make a list of planners, and since it wasn't yet two in the afternoon, he'd visit them all today and get estimates.

How hard could it be to find someone to put together a wedding that's a full month away?

❧

Bliss sank into the nearly scalding water and inhaled the warm scent of vanilla. She'd splurged on the bath products, but considering she'd never been one to shop much or spend a lot of money on herself, she justified the purchase as acceptable.

After all, in the two weeks since the Cake Bake had been open, Bliss had already surpassed the amount of sales she'd estimated in her business plan. Only the thought of what would happen should she give in to her penchant for overworking made her keep to her vow of doing no more than one wedding per week.

She blew out a long breath and watched the bubbles ripple and part, then lifted her right leg and rested her pink painted toes on the edge of the tub. Pedicures were her other weakness, one she'd decided was almost a necessity back when she was on her feet twelve hours a day in her capacity as executive chef.

Now pedicures and vanilla bath salts had become luxuries. Or were they part of her recovery? Probably so.

The scar that started on the inside of her knee had faded, but the evidence of her accident would never completely disappear. The marathons she used to run were a thing of the past, but given time and physical therapy, she might once again be running a 10k instead of contenting herself with walking to and from the market. Bliss sighed. For now, that would have to be enough.

The phone rang, and she rolled to her side to make a grab for it. Her mother's number blinked onto the caller ID, and for a second, Bliss thought of letting voice mail catch the call. Daughterly duty, or perhaps the fact she knew her mother would get in the car and drive over, compelled her to answer the phone.

While Mama made small talk about the weather, her Bible study lesson, and the status of her garden, Bliss clicked on the speakerphone and reached for her towel. By the time she slipped into her pink poodle pajamas and began cleaning her face, Bliss had begun to wonder the purpose for her mother's call.

"So, darling, I understand you're doing the cake for the Vincent wedding."

Bliss worked makeup remover onto her cheeks, then swiped at it with a cotton pad. "Two of them, actually," she said. "I've got Laura Vincent's wedding in March and Carolyn Vincent's in May."

"Oh my," her mother said. "I had no idea both sisters were engaged. And what a coup for you to get both weddings."

"Yes," Bliss said while stifling a giggle, "two Vincents. It's quite a coup."

"Honey." The warning tone in Mama's voice was unmistakable. "You aren't overdoing it, are you? You know what the doctors said."

Irritation flared, but Bliss clamped down on the feeling.

Mama had earned the right to ask such a question. She dabbed at her face, then snagged the moisturizer.

"Yes, I know, and I'm keeping to the schedule I agreed to. Monday, Wednesday, and Fridays from ten to four, and once a month, I work four hours on Saturday." She paused. "In fact, I've already turned away two potential customers because I couldn't fit them in."

"You did?" Relief flooded her mother's tone. "I'm glad to hear you're not. . .I mean, what with the other thing. . ."

Bliss stopped rubbing her face and frowned. This time her irritation won out. "It's okay, Mama. You can say it. Aneurysm. In addition to my bum knee, I have an aneurysm."

"A small one, but oh my, I think sometimes of how bad things could have been if you hadn't had the accident and had to get that MRI." Bliss could hear Mama suck in a breath, then let it out again. "Let's not talk about this, honey. Long as you're following doctor's orders, that thing—"

"Aneurysm."

"Yes, well, *that*. Anyway, it won't be a problem."

Bliss wiped her hands on the towel, then tossed it into the hamper. Regret tinged with love for her mother softened her voice. "Look, I'm sorry. It's just that I cannot let myself be afraid of my condition. I've never backed away from anything, and I'm not going to let this thing—"

"Aneurysm, honey."

Bliss shook her head as she chuckled. "Yes, I'm not going to let this aneurysm go unchecked. It's small. It's under control. And the minute that changes, the doctors are prepared to remove it. Now, how about I treat you to dinner tomorrow after work? We can have that crawfish pie you like so much."

"Oh, honey, that would be lovely. Can I bring anything?"

"Just yourself. Now go on to bed and stop worrying about me. I'm a grown woman, and I'm listening to my doctors. If it'll make you feel better, you can come along with me to New

Iberia next month for my checkup. Would you like that?"

"I would, honey," Mama said, "but not for the reason you think."

"Oh? What's the reason then?"

Bliss snapped off the bathroom light and padded down the hall to the front window. The tiniest sliver of a moon grazed the tips of the ancient magnolia at the corner. Four streets over, Mama most likely sat in her recliner with the shopping network on mute.

"I consider every day since your accident a gift," her mother said. "Spending a whole day with you, well, that would just be lovely. I don't seem to have much to fill my hours anymore. Not since we sold the sawmill."

She had to consider a second how to respond to this rare admission of Mama's loneliness. "Have you thought about going back to work somewhere, Mama?"

"Work?" Mama said. "Who would want to hire an old woman like me? Besides, if I worked, I'd miss that appointment with you. And I couldn't miss that. I'm looking forward to it already."

"And it doesn't hurt that your favorite shoe store's around the corner from the hospital, does it?"

Her mother's laughter put Bliss in mind of a woman far younger than the one now holding the other phone. She pulled the cord to lower the blinds and smiled.

"Shame on you, Bliss." Another giggle and a long pause. "That *is* about the time they put on their big spring sale, now that you mention it."

"Oh, Mama, may you never change," she whispered a few minutes later after hanging up. "And may I never take a day for granted again."

The next morning, she carried that thought to work and smiled when she recalled Mama's shoe sale comment. She had inherited her penchant for fancy footwear from her mother.

Unfortunately, the pair Bliss had chosen today pinched as much as they sparkled. As soon as she had the batter mixed up for Lizzie Spartman's red velvet cake and the timer set for the half dozen pumpkin breads the church ordered for Wednesday's women's event, Bliss kicked off the pretty pumps and donned a more comfortable pair of leopard-patterned velvet slippers.

She padded through the rest of the morning in those slippers, then made a sandwich and waited for the red velvet cake to cool. A hazard of her profession was tasting the goods, and rich cream cheese frosting was her favorite.

"Maybe just a smidge to be sure it's fit to sell." Bliss dipped a teaspoon in the icing, then lifted it to her mouth. It was every bit as good as she expected, tasty enough, in fact, to have just one more. . . .

"Bliss?"

The spoon clattered to the floor, and Bliss bent to retrieve it. "Hey, I haven't see you in a week, Neecie." She tossed the spoon into the sink and wiped her hands on the corner of her apron. "Come on back. I was just making lunch. Have you. . ." Neecie appeared in the doorway holding her cell phone to her chest, a stunned look on her face. "Oh my, what's wrong?"

"Wrong?" Neecie shook her head. "Nothing's wrong."

"Maybe you ought to sit down." Bliss gestured toward the nearest stool. "You look like you're about to keel over."

"No, I'm fine, really. I just wondered if you might, well. . ." Neecie clutched the phone tighter. "I've closed up the shop for the afternoon." She thrust the phone at Bliss. "The only reason this will ring is in case of a bridal emergency."

Bliss caught the phone after bobbling it twice. "But I don't understand. I thought you threw that sign away years ago."

"I made a new sign." Neecie jumped off the stool and shook her head, then closed the distance between them to embrace Bliss. "You always were dependable. I owe you one, Bliss."

Before Bliss could protest, Neecie was gone.

three

Exactly 4:00 p.m.

Bliss turned the OPEN sign over and locked the door. This Wednesday afternoon had been quiet—a half dozen telephone inquiries as to the costs of cakes and two orders for summer-time weddings.

Thankfully, Neecie's phone only rang once, and it was a wrong number. Bliss glanced over at the phone, now sitting atop the glass case beside the cash register.

"I wonder if Neecie's back from wherever she went in such a hurry."

She leaned forward to study the smattering of cars still parked at the curb in the hopes her friend's blue SUV would be there.

It wasn't.

"Wherever you are, I hope everything's all right," she said as she flipped off the lights and padded over the old floorboards toward the kitchen in her leopard slippers, her calendar under her arm. As an afterthought, she returned for Neecie's phone, placing it on the counter as she filled her teakettle.

She hadn't taken a walk in almost a week, and the lack of exercise showed in the stiffness of her knee and the beginnings of an ache in her back. While she waited, Bliss rose to reach for the tin of Earl Grey tea. Mission accomplished, she eased onto the stool and rested her feet on the opposite seat and let out a contented sigh.

Much as she missed her days running the kitchen at the Bentley, there was something to be said for sitting quietly and waiting for water to boil. As if on cue, the phone rang. Bliss nearly fell off the stool scrambling for it.

"Cake Bake," she said before she heard the dial tone and realized the ringing had come from Neecie's phone.

The phone rang again. "Oh, right. It's Neecie's."

Her palm closed over the still-jangling phone, and she punched the button, then lifted it to her ear. "Cake Bake, um, I mean Wedding Belles."

"Oh, thank the Lord. I thought you weren't going to answer." The deep voice held more than a note of urgency. "Now open up before I huff and puff and blow the house down."

"Blow the house down? Oh my."

With her heart pounding and her hands shaking, Bliss tiptoed over the creaking floorboards to the door and peered out in the direction of the sidewalk in front of Wedding Belles. A broad-shouldered man in jeans and a brown leather jacket stood with his back to her. He had dark, disheveled hair and a phone pressed against his ear.

Something about him seemed familiar. Of course, in Latagnier, everything and everyone was familiar. The fellow could be anyone from a distant cousin to an ax murderer.

Okay, so he wasn't carrying an ax. Still, he could be trouble.

And he could be a stranger. Despite the fact most traffic turned off at places like New Iberia or Lafayette before they ever reached Latagnier, a few were known to stray farther south.

And he did say he would blow the house down. Could his statement mean he'd resort to violence to get inside Neecie's shop?

Maybe he's a bill collector. Or an ex-boyfriend.

Whoever he was, the word *trouble* still seemed the best description. With that in mind, Bliss moved slowly toward the kitchen and the store phone she'd left on the counter.

The 911 system hadn't yet arrived in Latagnier, but on Bliss's first night in town, Mama had made her input the police station's number into her speed dial at the shop and upstairs on her home phone. She'd done the honors of saving the number to her cell phone herself.

Better to remain in sight of the stranger than to risk disappearing into the kitchen for even a minute. "Thank you, Mama," she whispered as she patted her apron pocket and felt for her cell phone.

"Did you say something?" The man heaved a sigh that she could hear and see, and Bliss's heart did a flip-flop. Yes, definitely trouble.

"Neecie, are you all right?" Mr. Trouble said. "You sound different. Something wrong with your voice?"

She watched him walk toward a big dark truck, one of those cowboy conveyances that gave no heed to the price of gas, and lean against the bumper. When he turned back in her direction, mirrored sunglasses glinting in the afternoon sun, Bliss ducked away from the window.

"What? No, I'm sorry." Bliss paused. What was wrong with her? "This is, well, I'm not her. Not Neecie, that is."

While she watched, he retrieved a briefcase, then slammed the door. "If you're not Neecie, then who are you?" he said when he returned to the sidewalk. "I need to talk to Neecie."

"This is her, um, emergency service."

Mr. Trouble set the briefcase on the sidewalk and now stood in front of the truck, one booted foot resting on the bumper. He seemed to be contemplating the toe of that boot, or maybe the bumper beneath it.

The man ran his free hand through his slightly-too-long hair and studied the toe of his boot. "Well, then, I'm in luck, because I've got an emergency."

"All right." Bliss ducked as the stranger's gaze swung her way. "Leave me your number, and I'll have Neecie call you back."

"No!"

The harshness of the man's tone made Bliss jump for cover. She looked up to check that the lock was secure on the door, then returned her attention to the caller, ignoring the twinge of complaint from her knee and the beginnings of the tea-kettle's whistle.

"Look, pal." Bliss swallowed hard and called to mind the difficult customers she'd dealt with in Austin. "I'm going to ask you once more. Do you want to leave a number or not?"

"No, I—"

Bliss clicked the phone off, her heart pounding. "Neecie Trahan, who in the world is this guy?" she whispered. "I hope he's not someone you're considering dating, because he really needs to learn some—"

Knock. Knock. Knock. "Anyone here?"

The man was back, and this time he'd come to her store instead of Neecie's place. What to do?

If she stood and ran toward the back, he could see her. The sound of the teakettle grew louder, giving her no choice but to jump up and skitter toward the kitchen.

"Hey, I see you in there." The knocking grew louder. "Please answer the door. It's an emergency. I'm looking for your neighbor Neecie. Have you seen her? Hey, come on. I said it was an emergency, and I'm not kidding."

"It's going to be an emergency, all right." Bliss lifted the teakettle from the stove and turned off the burner. "One more knock and I'm calling the law."

With shaking hands, Bliss prepared her daily cup of Earl Grey and settled onto the stool. From her vantage point, she could see the alley and the iron steps leading up to the second floor. Thankfully, the back door was barred and bolted during the day, so there was no chance the troublesome fellow would be coming in through that door.

The front entrance, well, that was another story. Bliss closed her eyes and prayed the Lord would send someone to diffuse the situation and cause Mr. Trouble to go about his merry way. Or, rather, his cranky way.

He did seem to be a volatile sort.

A quarter hour passed, and Bliss finished her tea in silence. After washing the cup and setting it to drain on the sideboard, she decided to brave a peek outside. Sliding across the wooden planks on tiptoe, she kept to the shadows and never allowed her gaze to move from the front window.

So far, the only signs of life were from the few cars that traveled downtown after four. There was certainly no sign of the troublemaker with the mirrored shades.

Bliss expelled an audible breath as she checked the clock. Four thirty. Time to start supper. Mama always liked to eat early. At least the prep time today was minimal. She'd put the crawfish pie together earlier. Now all that remained to be done was to put it in the oven for an hour of baking time.

"Mission accomplished," she said as she set the timer. "Now what to do?" Her gaze landed on the calendar, and she retrieved it. "Let's see what next week looks like. Maybe I can get a head start on the list for the grocery store."

Ten minutes later, she'd made notes on items to purchase at the market and updated her calendar on her computer. A neat calendar filled with dates and deadlines, as well as the details of each event, spilled from her printer, and she caught it before it landed on the floor.

Tacking the thing on the fridge with a big crawfish-shaped magnet, Bliss took a step backward and stared at the page. Two weeks in business and she was completely booked through April with the month of May nearly full, as well.

Bliss let out a contented sigh. For all the complaining she had done since the accident, the Lord had come through for her.

"As if He wouldn't, silly," she said aloud.

But there had been so many times when she felt sure He'd forgotten all about her. Terrible times of doubt followed moments of anger over the fact that God let her hit that patch of ice, that He had allowed her car to go through it rather than around it.

That He had sent her through this new phase of her life rather than around it.

She glanced down at her slippers and wiggled her toes. Back at the Bentley, she'd be barking orders in high heels.

Perhaps there was something to be said for following the Lord's plan rather than your own. "To say the least," Bliss whispered. "Father, forgive me for fighting You on this." She touched the calendar, then let her finger trail down the cold length of the refrigerator door. "Next time, stop me, okay? I'd rather You be in charge, even if I don't always act like it."

Neecie's phone rang, and Bliss nearly jumped out of her skin. She peered out the kitchen, past the display cases, and toward the front door.

The phone rang again. Bliss took a step toward it.

No one appeared in the door, and no ranting males seemed to be pacing the sidewalk. She picked it up on the third ring, prepared for battle.

"Bliss, it's Neecie."

"Oh, Neecie." Bliss felt her shoulders slump. "I'm so glad to hear from you. Is everything all right? Are you all right?"

"I'm fine." She paused. "I'm sorry I ran out like that earlier. I really appreciate you minding the store for me. Did everything go okay?"

"Pretty much." Bliss cast another glance outside. "There was this man. Irate fellow, actually. He demanded to speak to you. Said it was a wedding emergency." An idea dawned. "Hey, you weren't playing a joke on me, were you?"

Neecie giggled. "No," she said, "but it would've been a good one. Did this man say who he was?"

"No, he just kept asking for you. I tried to get him to leave a number, but he wouldn't do it."

"That's odd."

"Yeah." She considered her words as she spoke. "Neecie, is there something wrong? Something I can help with?"

Her friend sighed audibly. "I wish you could, hon. Keeping an eye on the phone was a big help."

"Anytime."

"Yes, well, you're closed this Saturday, aren't you?"

"I am." The smell of crawfish pie made Bliss's stomach growl. She padded toward the kitchen to check the progress of her dinner. "I'll be open two Saturdays from now. I decided it's easier for customers to remember I'm open the first Saturday of the month and closed the rest of them. Don't you think?"

"Yes, of course." Her response sounded rushed. "Bliss, I wonder if I could trouble you to slip the phone through the mail slot. I would send Hannah or one of the boys over, but—"

"Oh, there's no need for that. I'll drop it in." She closed the oven door. "You just enjoy your evening and call me if you need anything else, you hear?"

"I will, hon." She paused. "And, Bliss?"

"What's that, Neecie?"

"I'm really glad you're home."

"Me, too," she said as she hung up. And, strangely, she meant it.

Now to take the phone back before she forgot.

❧

Finally.

It didn't take a genius to know that if he waited long enough, the woman from the cake store would emerge. Bob hadn't yet figured out why this gal had possession of Neecie's phone, but he aimed to ask Neecie come Sunday morning. He also planned to tell her she needed to find someone more professional to handle her calls.

Either that or hire a temp when she couldn't be there.

At the thought of hiring a temp, Bob suppressed a groan. He couldn't wait to welcome Yvonne back. Come next

Monday, life would be good again. He would be at work, and Yvonne would take care of everything else.

Today, however, he still had the matter of Amy's wedding to handle.

The woman still stood in the doorway of the Cake Bake. Bob eased down in his seat and adjusted his collar as he watched her through his aviator shades. It wouldn't do to scare her again. He'd have to make his move slowly, deliberately.

Losing the last link to his mission was something he could not do. Especially since Neecie and everyone else associated with Amy's wedding seemed to have gone AWOL.

The woman closed the shop door and, curiously, walked away without locking it. "Must have one of those old-fashioned door locks," he muttered. "Figures someone not smart enough to answer the phone right wouldn't know about proper security, either."

Keeping to the edge of the sidewalk closest to the building, the woman eased her way over to the door of Neecie's shop. She ignored the door handle and instead pressed on the mail slot.

"What's she doing?"

The woman seemed to be trying to jam something into the slot. Something black, it seemed from the place where he'd moved his truck. Bob leaned forward a bit to get a better look. That's when she spied him.

Knowing he was well and truly caught, Bob took the only alternative open to him. He swung open the truck door. "Hey, you there. Excuse me, but I need to talk to you a second."

Wide eyes turned to collide with his gaze. The woman gave the black thing one last shove with her palm, then made an odd squeaking noise and skittered back toward the cake shop.

"Wait. Don't go." He lunged from the truck and dodged the parking meter to try and catch up to her. Just as she slipped inside, Bob stuck his foot in to keep the door from shutting.

That was his first mistake.

four

Bliss pressed her shoulder against the door and held the man pinned in place while she fumbled with Neecie's phone. Where was her cell when she needed it?

"I'm calling the police," she said as she tried to dial the number. "I'd advise you to leave."

"I'm sorry, ma'am, but I can't do that," the man said. "My foot is stuck."

She looked down and saw that what he said was true. She also saw the only way to release him would then free him to come barging through the door.

"I can't let you go until the police come." For emphasis, she banged her palm on the door.

"Police?" He gave her a stricken look. "As if my day isn't going down the tubes already. Why in the world would you feel the need to call the police?"

"You might come back and attack me again."

Bliss braced herself against the door and punched a number she hoped would ring at the police station. If only she'd thought to bring her cell phone with her. Fat lot of good it did her sitting on the kitchen counter.

The phone rang twice. "Flower shop."

"Oops, sorry. Wrong number." Bliss hung up the phone and gave the door another shove.

"Ouch." The door rattled as he yanked at the foot she held trapped. "Don't be ridiculous. I didn't attack you. If anything, *you* attacked me."

"I did nothing of the sort." She glared at him through the front door's wavy glass. "What would you do if a stranger harassed you on a public sidewalk?"

The man's expression softened. "I didn't mean to harass you, but if you perceived it that way, then I apologize."

She frowned. "Apology accepted. But there's still the matter of who you are. You wouldn't even leave a callback number for Neecie."

"I thought you were joking. Everyone in three counties knows me. If you've flown a plane. . ." He paused to try and wriggle his foot out of the trap. "If you've got crops to be dusted or a package to be delivered, chances are you've dealt with Tratelli Aviation. Now, come on and let me go. I promise I'll leave."

"Tratelli Aviation?" Bliss blinked hard and once again peered out the door at the man she held captive.

She studied the broad-shouldered man through the wavy glass. The Bobby Tratelli she knew was a chubby kid with a stutter and unforgettable blue eyes who spent all his time in his best friend, Landon's, shadow. While Landon threw touchdown passes and made passes at girls, Bobby blocked for him—on and off the field.

The man on the other side of the door looked as if he'd never been out of the spotlight. Perhaps the company was sold to new owners. That would certainly explain the fact that other than the color of his hair, this man did not resemble the annoying pest she'd tried to ignore all through school.

"Hey, Bliss Denison? Is that you?"

"Yes," she said slowly.

He adjusted his shades and gave a curt nod. "I heard you were back in town."

She tilted her chin, still distrustful.

"Hey, Bliss, remember that time in junior high when you dared Landon and me to climb in the back window and spend the night inside the sawmill?"

Her eyes narrowed. How did this man know about that?

"You told us the dog would eat us if he caught us, but by morning, we had your grandpa's German shepherd fetching and rolling over." He paused to chuckle. "Best I can recall, that dog's name was Killer, at least until we tamed him. After that, I think old Mr. Denison just called him Trip." He paused. "I believe that stood for Trained Pet."

"Trip. He used to let me ride around on his back." She smiled. "Oh my. I haven't thought about that dog in years."

Then it hit her. Bliss swallowed hard. Her grasp on the door frame slipped, and she grabbed for the handle. If he knew about Trip, then he had to be. . .

"Bobby?" She shook her head. "Bobby Tratelli? Is that you?"

He lowered his shades and shrugged. "Yeah, it's me."

Even without the insider information on Grandpa's dog, Bliss would've known those eyes anywhere: denim blue with a rim of gold framed in lashes she'd teased him about in homeroom. But the muscles, the soft Southern drawl without a single misspoken word?

"Oh my," she said softly. "What happened to you?" Her gaze swept the length of him. "You used to be, well. . .that is, you didn't look so. . .that is, you were. . ." Her words trailed off as heat flooded her cheeks.

Bobby seemed to understand. His grin broadened despite her faux pas. "The summer after graduation, I let my grandpa talk me into signing on for a location shoot on one of his movies. I thought I was going to be the next greatest thing in Hollywood. Turns out the picture was being shot in West Texas. I ended up playing a greenhorn cowboy on a working ranch. I had no idea how hard cowboys work."

"By the end of the summer, I'd decided I wasn't leaving Texas or the ranch life, and I didn't until Pop decided he needed me to take over for him at the company. When I came home for Christmas that year, I arrived in the middle of the night and snuck into my room, thinking I would surprise them in the morning. Mama called the cops because she thought a stranger had broken into the house and fallen asleep in my bed." He peered down at Bliss through the glass. "I'll tell you like I told my mother: It's me; there's just less of me to love."

Her heart did an idiotic flutter when Bobby broke into a crooked grin.

What was wrong with her? This was just Bobby Tratelli. The same Bobby Tratelli who followed Landon around like a lost puppy. The goofy guy who took great pleasure in teasing her about everything from her short stature to that store-bought perm her mama insisted would give her straight locks more body.

Bobby gestured to the ground. "Say, considering we're old friends and all, do you think maybe you could let me in? That door's starting to pinch a bit."

"Oh! I'm so sorry." She jumped back and opened the door. "Please, come in."

❧

Bob rolled into the store shoulder first, then found his balance and landed on his feet. When he straightened up, he caught sight of bead board walls and a broad expanse of counters in matching cypress wood that made the space look more like his grandma Breaux's old-fashioned kitchen than a store.

A giant brass chandelier that he recognized from the old Latagnier Bank hung from the ceiling and lit a table covered with baked goods in the center of the room. To his right was a wall of shelves lined with more of the same, interspersed with what looked like antique photographs of Latagnier.

"Care for some coffee?"

Bob tore his attention from a picture of his dad standing beside a 1940s vintage P-51 aircraft with a Flying Tigers logo beneath the front propeller. "Coffee? Sure." He paused. "Say, where did you get this picture?"

Bliss walked over to stand beside him, then leaned over to

look at the photograph. Wow, she smelled good.

"Oh, I remember this one." She pulled a pair of reading glasses from her shirt pocket and reached for the picture. "I think it came out of the old VFW Hall. I got a whole box of things when they moved into their new facilities." A look of recognition crossed her face, and she glanced up at Bob. "Say, isn't this your dad?"

"It is," Bob said.

The smile on her face made her brown eyes sparkle. "I'd love it if you'd take it," she said.

"What? No, I couldn't," he said, although he really would have liked to have a copy of it.

"I insist." She pressed the frame into his hand and winked. "I dare you."

Bob laughed out loud. "I never could resist one of your dares, Bliss."

He followed behind Bliss Denison until he smelled the candles. His nose began to tingle, and he had to stop. "Do I smell vanil—"

A sneeze stopped him in midsentence.

When Bliss turned around, he pointed to the offending item: a fat, white, three-wicked candle situated in the middle of a bunch of white flowers on the glass-topped counter. Another sneeze nearly blew the blossoms off the table.

Bliss seemed to understand. A moment later, she'd blown out the candle and headed toward the back of the shop.

"I'm sorry about that," she said over her shoulder. "I forget that some people are allergic to fragrance."

"Not all," he managed as he waved away the acrid-smelling wisps of candle smoke and slipped into the kitchen a step behind Bliss. "Just vanilla ones." He shrugged. "Can't explain it. My wife used to burn all sorts of those things in the house, and it didn't do a thing to me. Guess she never got around to vanilla."

Bliss nodded but did not respond. Rather, she reached for a matching pair of white oven mitts with a red pepper logo on them. "Give me a second to check this, and then I'll get to that coffee."

Bob leaned on the door frame and took in the room. One side seemed to be given over to appliances and cooking spaces, while the other side hosted a cypress sideboard filled with flowery plates and a table of the same pale wood with ornately carved legs and four matching chairs. Something about the dining set seemed vaguely familiar.

"Have a seat." Bliss gestured to one of two stools parked near the white-painted cabinets.

She opened the top door of an industrial-sized wall oven and stood on tiptoe to lift a piece of foil off a pie plate. When she did, a tantalizing scent drifted toward him.

To Bob's horror, his stomach growled. Bliss must have heard, because she sent him a sideways glance as she closed the oven door.

"Hungry?" She chuckled. "Why don't you stay for supper? I've got plenty of crawfish pie for all three of us."

All three of us? Bob frowned. Was he intruding on a date?

"Oh no," he said quickly, "I couldn't possibly interrupt your evening."

"My evening? Oh, please." Bliss balled up the foil and tossed it toward the sink, hitting it dead center. "My evening consists of me listening to my mother tell stories about the quilt ladies and her volunteer work at the hospital. Since Mama tends to run out of original material and repeat herself, I would welcome that interruption. I'd also like to know what you've been up to since graduation, besides your career as a cowboy."

He pretended to consider his options for a second. "Sounds like an offer I can't refuse."

"Good," she said as she reached into the freezer and pulled

out a container of coffee grounds. As the freezer door shut, she wagged her finger at him. "Just don't tell me I didn't warn you when Mama starts telling her tales. She can go all night on the good old days. By that, I mean the magical years before the Cineplex and cable television came to Latagnier."

Bob settled himself on the nearest stool and made an X over his heart. "I promise."

While Bliss busied herself at the coffeepot, Bob took the opportunity to study his old friend. Back in junior high, she'd played Becky Thatcher to his and Landon's Tom and Huck. Any adventure they'd concocted, Bliss managed to top.

And the dares. How many times had an innocent "I dare you" turned an adventure into a week's worth of punishment from their parents?

Bob chuckled. Funny how Bliss never managed to get caught.

She plugged in an ancient coffeepot, then turned to give him a look. "What're you smiling about?"

"Just thinking about old times."

Bliss crossed her arms over her chest and frowned. "Well, keep them to yourself, would you? Mama doesn't know half of the adventures I had, and I'd hate to send her over the edge at her advanced age."

"Advanced age? I heard that, Chambliss Rose, and you'd be surprised to find out just how much of your storied past I do know about."

"Chambliss Rose?" Bob shook his head. "I've known you since third grade and never had any idea that was your real name."

Bliss switched off the oven and reached for the mitts again. As she opened the oven door, the room flooded with the smell of crawfish pie.

"That's because Mama promised she wouldn't make me answer to that name. It belonged to my great-grandmother

Denison, and Daddy was set on keeping it in the family tree. Something about my grandma Dottie only having boys. Anyway, Mama, however, wasn't so keen on it. In fact, every year before school started, she would have a talk with my teacher and ask her to call me Bliss." Bliss paused to rest her hand on her hip. "She only trots it out when she's trying to make a point."

"Advanced age, indeed," her mother muttered before crossing the room to envelop Bob in a hug. "How are you, Bobby?" she asked.

"Couldn't be better," he said, "except for this twinge here." He pointed to his boot and tried not to grin. "It's paining me a bit this evening."

Mrs. Denison's gray brows knitted in concern as she dropped her handbag onto the counter and removed her red coat and matching gloves. "What did you do to that foot of yours, hon?"

"Got it caught in a door," he said as he slid a sly wink toward Bliss.

"Bobby Tratelli, I thought you'd left your awkward days after high school." Bliss's mother shook her head. "How in the world did you manage to get your foot caught in the door?"

"Food's ready," Bliss interrupted. She gave Bob a stern look before turning her attention to her mother. "Mama, why don't you hand me those plates, and I'll dish us up some crawfish pie. Bobby, if you wouldn't mind fetching three tea glasses off the sideboard, I've got sweet tea ready to pour." She shrugged. "Or I can pour you the coffee I promised you."

"Sweet tea's fine."

Bob grinned and let the subject change. Before he knew what had happened, his belly was full and he'd just finished stabbing his fork into the last bite of ice cream covered peach cobbler on his plate.

He'd also been entertained with Mrs. Denison's stories of

life in Latagnier back before cable television and the Cineplex ruined the place. In her opinion, anyway.

"And so you see," Bliss's mother continued, "your mama's family and ours go way back. I'd say it all started with that sawmill and your uncle Ernest. This is one of his tables, isn't it, Bliss?"

"It is. The chairs, too, I think. At least that's what I've been told." Bliss set the coffeepot in the center of the table, then turned her attention to Bob. "Want some more cobbler, Bobby?"

"I don't know where I'd put it, but thanks all the same." He pushed away and set his fork down as the clock began to strike the hour. Where had the time gone?

Mrs. Denison looked up from her dessert and seemed to be counting the chimes, as well. When they stopped at seven, she glanced over at Bob. "So, I hear tell you're having a wedding in your family soon."

"The wedding!" Bob nearly fell off the stool. "I almost forgot why I stopped by. My daughter's getting married, and I'm looking for someone to take care of the details."

"A pity her mama's not here to handle that," Mrs. Denison said.

"Yes, ma'am," he said. "I imagine Karen would have been right in the middle of all this. Probably butting heads with Amy since she's too much like me."

"Yes." Bliss's mother smiled. "What with Amy flying those planes and working beside you as if she were a son, she's a girl after her daddy's own heart."

"A father couldn't ask for a better child, that's for sure," he responded, suddenly missing his dark-haired princess. He'd give Amy a call when he left for home just so he could hear her voice. With any luck, she wouldn't ask about the wedding.

"Bobby, when's the wedding?" Bliss asked.

"A month from tomorrow."

Her brows shot up, and she nearly dropped her coffee cup. "Are you telling me your daughter is getting married a month from tomorrow and you're just now planning the wedding? I sure hope it's a small one."

He sighed. "Last I heard we had over four hundred responses to the invitations."

"Four hundred responses?" Bliss's eyes widened. "You must've sent out a thousand invitations."

"You've got to take into account all our business associates." Bob frowned. "Twelve hundred invitations, I think."

"You don't know?" Bliss reached for the coffeepot and poured herself a cup as if to steady her nerves. "One thousand two hundred people have been invited to your daughter's wedding and you only know the date?"

Bob shrugged. "Amy had it under control. I just wrote the checks."

Mrs. Denison reached over to lay her hand atop his. "Then what happened, hon?"

"Then she left two weeks ago. It was all *under control*. That's what she said."

Bliss's mother patted his hand again. "Well, then I'm sure it is. What's the worry?"

"The worry is the wedding planner has run off with the plans." When the woman looked confused, he tried again. "He couldn't be reached by phone, so I made a trip to Baton Rouge. The shop was locked up tight with a notice from the law on the door."

"That's not good," Mrs. Denison said.

"No, it's not. I tried every planner in Baton Rouge, but when I told them the wedding was a month away, they all laughed me out of their shops. I couldn't call my daughter because she'd worry, and my mother's in California until the end of the month. I know I've got more cousins than the law ought to allow, but I can't think of one of them that I'd trust to run a wedding of this size."

Bliss's mother nodded her agreement. "Not only that, but when you involve one member of the family, you generally get them all. It'd be rule by committee, and that's just another word for organized chaos."

"Sounds like you've been to the Breaux Thanksgiving dinner." Bob exhaled and tried to shrug the stiffness from his neck. "Yes, well, anyway, I thought since Amy got her dress from Neecie, maybe she could get the rest of the wedding there, too." He paused. "Do you happen to know where she is?"

Bliss shook her head. "Neecie didn't say where she was going, but she left her phone, then lit out of here in a hurry. I really thought she'd be back before the end of the business day, but when she phoned, she didn't say what time or even if she'd return."

"Well how about that?" Mrs. Denison pushed a peach slice around on her plate with the back of her fork.

"Mama," Bliss said slowly, "is there something you're not telling me?"

"If I weren't telling you, then I couldn't say I was, could I?"

"That makes absolutely no sense." Bliss gave her mother a look. "Mama, you're hiding something."

Bob reached for the coffeepot. He'd lived with a daughter long enough to know things were about to get more than a little bit interesting.

five

"I'm not hiding a thing, Bliss," Mama said. "I just don't know if I know anything, so I'm going to keep my mouth shut about it."

"That doesn't make a lick of sense, Mama."

"Well, it'll have to do for now." Mama swung her gaze from the peach slice she'd been studying to their guest. "The real concern here is with Bobby. Looks like he's up a creek without a paddle as far as this wedding he's paying for goes." She shook her finger at him. "How in the world did you end up with a wedding that big and no one to run things a month before the big day?"

Poor guy. Bobby looked like he'd been hit with a wet dishrag right between the eyes. He certainly never saw that change of topic coming. Bliss, on the other hand, fully expected her mother wouldn't spill whatever news she had on the first attempt and would use any means to avoid questions. Changing the subject was her favorite tactic.

Just wait until Bobby Tratelli went home. Mama would be talking before she knew what happened. Once Bliss got Neecie's story out of her, she'd start quizzing Mama about why Bobby kept referring to his wife in the past tense. Much as she wanted to know, Bliss hadn't figured out a polite way to ask.

"Best as I can tell, it happened like this. First, Amy. . ." He looked over at Bliss. "That's my daughter." When Bliss nodded, he continued. "The contract she'd been negotiating finally got set for signing. Trouble is, the other parties are in London and the deal had to be completed before the wedding."

47

"Oh no," Bliss said. "I can't imagine having to leave with such an important event on the horizon."

Bobby's gaze collided with hers. "I agree, but Amy didn't seem worried in the least. Said everything was under control." He shook his head. "She went over expecting to spend a week or two and then get right back here. Last night she called to say it would be another week."

"That's not so bad, is it?" Mama asked. "That still leaves plenty of time until the big day. Or could it be you miss your girl?"

Bobby seemed to consider the question a minute. "Honestly, Mrs. Denison, I'll be happier when my daughter's back home and this wedding is nothing but a sweet memory and a bunch of pretty pictures in a scrapbook." He paused. "So, yes, even though this wedding's driving me to distraction, I have to admit I do miss my little girl." Bobby smiled. "Not that she's so little anymore, of course."

Bliss felt the old tug of regret on her heart, the one that reminded her that while she was climbing her way up the corporate ladder, she'd climbed right past the place where babies and a family were. Her reward was to be left without either: no career and no family. Well, other than Mama and her numerous opinionated but lovable cousins.

"What exactly do you need done, Bobby?" Mama asked.

"That's the trouble." Bobby scrubbed his face with the palms of his hands. "I'm still trying to piece all that together. If my assistant weren't in Hawaii, I'd probably have better luck following that paper trail."

"You poor dear," Mama said. "Although I must tell you how wonderful it was of you to send Yvonne and Jack on that vacation. She talked of nothing else but that trip at the quilt guild meetings for weeks." She paused to toy with her napkin. "I must say a body could get jealous if she were of a mind to. After all, I've got more than twenty-five years at my job."

"I didn't know you had a job, Mrs. Denison." Bobby gave her his full attention. "What is it you do?"

"Why, I'm mama to Bliss, of course," she said, sweet as pie. "I'd think that ought to get me at least a weekend in some place other than Latagnier, if not three weeks in Hawaii."

Bliss shook her head. If she didn't know Mama so well, she might get her feelings hurt. This, however, was her mother's way of teasing. She could tell it from the gleam in Mama's eyes. No one could keep a straight face like Mama.

Of course, Bliss could give as good as she got. After all, she'd learned from the master.

"Well, that's a good thing to know," Bliss said. "To think I was going to send you on that quilt cruise to Alaska this summer for your birthday." She feigned relief. "Now I can save my money and put you up for a weekend at the Snooze On Inn over in New Iberia, knowing you'll be just as happy there."

Mama looked to be thinking of a retort, then seemed to reconsider. She gave Bliss a wink before patting Bobby's hand again. "So, ignore my daughter, Bobby, and tell me about your problem at work."

"My problem at work." Bobby dipped his head. "Well, Mrs. Denison, I'm afraid my good intentions are backfiring on me. I can't find a thing in the office, I've been through three temps in the two weeks since Yvonne left, and right now I've got no one."

Mama cast Bliss a sideways glance. "Do you need some help, Bobby?"

"Help?"

He looked confused, so Bliss decided to come to his aid. "Mama's offering to come work at your office until Yvonne gets back," she supplied. "When Daddy took the sawmill over from Granddad, Mama kept his books and ran the office."

Her friend's expression turned hopeful. "Seriously? You would do that?"

"Well, of course I would, young man. I wouldn't want my friend Yvonne to come back to a big mess. Now what time do you need me at work?"

"I, um, that is, Yvonne generally arrives around eight. If that's too early for you—"

"Too early?" Mama pushed back from the table and rose. "By eight o'clock I've cooked breakfast, cleaned house, and walked a mile around the track behind my house. If I skip the cleaning, I can be there by seven thirty."

"Mrs. Denison, I'll send someone to clean for you if you can get there that early."

While Mama seemed to be considering the offer, Bliss tried to keep from laughing out loud. Working for a week was exactly what Mama needed. Now maybe she'd stop babying Bliss.

At least temporarily.

"It's a deal," her mother finally said. "I guess I don't have to ask about the dress code or where to park my convertible."

"I'll trust you on both counts." Bobby rose and stuck his hand out to shake with Mama. "I sure do appreciate this."

Mama waved away the comment and reached for her coat. "Pshaw," she said as Bliss helped her shrug into the red wool number she'd been wearing for more than three decades of Louisiana winters. "You two young people don't stay up too late. Tomorrow's a workday, you know."

"Not for me, Mama," Bliss said as she placed the familiar well-worn red leather gloves in her mother's hands. "Tomorrow's Thursday. That's my day off."

"Good for you, honey," Mama said before making her good-byes to Bobby and linking arms with Bliss. "Walk me to the car, would you?"

"Sure, Mama," Bliss said.

"Why don't I help you to your car, Mrs. Denison?" Bobby asked.

"No, thank you, dear," her mother said sweetly. Too sweetly. "I'll be needing Bliss, but you're quite the gentleman for offering."

Bliss exchanged amused looks with Bobby, then pulled away from Mama's grasp to snag her wrap from the peg by the back door. "Will you excuse us a minute?" she said. "I'll be right back."

Something was up for sure. Mama never required an escort anywhere, much less to the front door. Any suggestion she might need help would have been met with a chuckle at best.

They got all the way out the front door of the shop and onto the sidewalk before Mama decided to come clean. "All right, Bliss," she said as she leaned toward her. "I think maybe Neecie's in trouble."

"What?"

"I didn't want to say anything in front of Bobby, but I don't think Neecie's going to be much help to him in planning that wedding."

"Why's that?"

Mama craned her neck back in the direction of the shop, then returned her attention to Bliss. "Well, it's funny how people think just because you qualify for a senior citizen discount that your ears don't work anymore."

Bliss waited, knowing her mother would eventually get to the point. From experience, she also knew that hurrying her only served to slow the woman down.

Once again, Mama inched toward her. "Especially in bathroom stalls. You'd never believe what's overheard in the ladies' room. Just let a woman get on a cell phone behind a closed door, and you'd be shocked at what's being said."

"Mama, I don't think gossip is an appropriate—"

"Nobody's gossiping here," came her sharp retort. "If you'd listen, you'd know that." She paused for effect. "Just this afternoon I was over at the Shoe Shack looking for some winter loafers. Well, the coffee got the best of me, and I had to excuse myself just as I was about to try on the most darling pair of periwinkle pumps."

"Really?" A chill wind teased the tails of her wrap, and Bliss gathered it tighter around her. *Hurry up, Mama.*

"So, as I was saying, there I was, a captive audience, so to speak, when I heard a familiar voice in the stall next to me."

"Neecie?" Bliss supplied.

"Yes, it was." Mama placed her hand atop Bliss's. "And, honey, she didn't sound happy at all. Whoever she was talking to was getting a piece of her mind. I'd say that was around one o'clock, give or take a few minutes."

"One o'clock? That's interesting. She dropped her phone off with me around noon, but I sure didn't get the impression she was going shoe shopping. I mean, she seemed awfully upset." Bliss shuddered. "What did you hear Neecie say?"

"Honey, I don't recall all of it, but she was giving someone a piece of her mind for causing her to close the store like she did. Mentioned you by name, too. Said she had to get her friend Bliss Denison to cover the phone and if the person on the line tried to call her at work they'd reach you. Then she said, 'Yes, *that* Bliss Denison,' whatever that meant."

"I have no idea."

"And then she said something really odd. I've tried to figure out what she meant, but then maybe I just didn't understand." Mama shook her head. "Someone flushed. Can you believe it?"

"Well, Mama, it *is* a bathroom." Bliss expelled a long breath. "So, what was the odd thing Neecie said?"

"She said, 'Maybe it's best for everyone if you just stay gone.' Least that's what it sounded like." Mama paused to search for her keys in the seemingly bottomless black leather purse she never left home without. "Oh, and there was something else. Neecie told whoever she was talking to that she'd already bought a plane ticket and it better not go to waste." She lifted a ring that looked more appropriate for a jailer than a senior citizen.

A car passed, and Mama waved, jingling the keys as she shook her arm. Bliss watched the taillights disappear around the corner as she pondered this piece of news.

"And you heard all of this in the shoe store ladies' room?"

"You'd be surprised at what you hear at a shoe store." She hit the button on the key ring, and her car chirped. "Something about trying on shoes. You love 'em as much as I do, but you miss the best part when you order online like you do. Go sit in a shoe store and see if I'm wrong."

"You sure we're talking about the same Shoe Shack?"

Mama chuckled. "Spoken like someone who has never experienced the healing properties of shoe shopping therapy done correctly." Before Bliss could comment, her mother held her hands up to silence her. "You know I'm kidding, of course. The only place I take my troubles is to the Lord." She paused. "Although I would venture to guess shoe shopping's not a bad way to get your mind off things once you've prayed and sought His counsel."

"Mama!"

"All right," she said as she took a step toward her car. "I'm going home now." After opening the door and settling behind the wheel, Mama pressed the button that rolled down the driver's side window. "Bliss, I might have misunderstood what Neecie said, but there was no misunderstanding her tone. That girl's scared of something."

Bliss thought back to earlier in the day and the look on her friend's face. "Yes, Mama, I think she might be."

"Then we need to be praying for her." Mama's window rolled back into place as the car disappeared into the night.

"I've already started," Bliss said as she watched the Buick's taillights disappear around the corner.

"Started what?" Bobby asked from the doorway.

Bliss jumped and whirled around to face him. "You scared the living daylights out of me, Bobby Tratelli."

"I'm sorry. I wasn't trying to spy," he said quickly. "I stayed back inside where I couldn't hear, but it's dark out. When your mother drove away, I was afraid, well. . ."

"It's all right." Bliss gathered her wrap close and smiled as she walked toward him. "Thank you," she said. "That was very nice of you."

Bobby looked surprised but said nothing. Rather, he stood tall and straight, his face partly hidden in the shadows. She looked up into his amazing eyes and wondered how so many years had flown by.

Somewhere along the way, she'd forgotten about Bobby and Landon and all the fun they'd had at Latagnier High. When did life get so—

"Bliss? You're staring at me."

"I am?" She blinked. "Yes, well, I guess I was. I'm sorry." A chill wind swirled past, and she nodded toward the door. "Would you like to come back in?"

Bobby stuffed his fists into the front pockets of his jeans and hunched his shoulders. "I'd better not."

"Are you sure?" Bliss shrugged. "With all the talking my mother did, I never got to hear what you've been up to all these years."

He seemed to consider the statement for a minute before shaking his head. "Much as I'd like to, I can't. Unlike certain people, I've got to get up and go to work tomorrow morning."

"Oh, c'mon," Bliss said. "You're the boss. Do you *have* to go to work early tomorrow?"

"Yes, I have to." He leaned down to give Bliss a quick hug. "You forget. Your mother will be there at the crack of dawn, most likely."

"All the more reason," she called after him as he trotted to his truck. "I generally try to steer clear of Mama until after she's had her second cup of coffee."

Bobby palmed his keys and glanced back over his shoulder. "Any particular reason?"

"I could tell you," Bliss responded, "but that would take all the fun out of it. Best you find out for yourself."

He froze.

"I'm just teasing you, Bobby." Bliss's laughter echoed in the quiet night. "My mother ran the sawmill for close to three decades. She'd probably still be out there if Daddy hadn't sold it and insisted the new owners leave Mama be. He figured he was helping her to enjoy her retirement."

Leaning against the hood of the truck, he watched Bliss's slim figure disappear into the shadows as she stepped out onto the sidewalk. Now all he could see was her silhouette, a small woman with curves in all the right places and hair that was tossed about in the breeze.

Strange, but it was all he could do not to request she take three steps in his direction so the streetlight would reveal her face again. Uncomfortable with the direction of his thoughts, Bob forced his attention back to the subject at hand.

"So, are you saying your mother isn't enjoying her retirement? Should I be worried that she might want to steal Yvonne's job away from her?"

"Stranger things have happened," was Bliss's cryptic comment.

"Well this could be awful. Yvonne's coming back to work a week from Monday." He feigned confusion and tried not to join Bliss in her giggling. "I could have a real catfight on my hands if your mother refuses to give Yvonne the job back."

Bliss stepped from the shadows and revealed a broad smile. "You could indeed."

Moonlight washed over her features and enhanced high cheekbones and the slight tilt to her nose. Bob thought to go back and repeat the innocent hug he'd given her, this time lingering a moment longer. Instead, his feet remained glued to the blacktop road, the only sensible solution.

After all, this was Bliss Denison. The same Bliss Denison who never looked directly at him because she was too busy trying to catch the eye of his best friend, Landon.

The same Bliss Denison he'd been secretly in love with since the third grade.

"You okay, Bobby?" She took another step forward. "You must be thinking that I've gotten you into all kinds of trouble."

Little did she know how much trouble he was in.

"You guessed it," he said as casually as he could manage. "So, now that you've got me into this mess, do you have any advice as to how to get me out of it?"

"Advice on how to handle my mother?" Again Bliss laughed. "How much time do you have?"

He looked up at the heavens, then down at his watch. "I ought to be heading home, but I could be tempted to stay for a cup of coffee and an hour of conversation. What do you think?"

From where he stood, he could see her nod. "Come on back inside, then. I'll make a fresh pot."

"No," he said quickly. From the look on her face—too quickly. "It's a beautiful night, and my guess is you've been cooped up in that kitchen all day. Am I right?"

Her smile was glorious. "Yes, that's true," she said slowly.

"Then let me have my turn offering you coffee. What say we stroll down to the Java Hut? My treat."

six

Stroll down to the Java Hut? That was four blocks away. Bliss bit her lip and thought only a moment before making her decision.

"Sure, but let me grab my coat. I'm shivering out here already."

Bobby looked concerned. "I could drive us."

Ah, a sensible solution, especially since she'd been on her feet all day. Bliss glanced up at the starry night, inhaled the crisp February air.

"No, it's fine."

And it was. The stroll down Main Street flew by, and before Bliss realized it, the Java Hut loomed ahead just the other side of the Magnolia Café.

They'd walked in silence, a fact that made Bliss smile. No need to force conversation with someone you'd known since pink bows and ruffled socks were a fashion statement. Since he and Landon were forced to buy her a new bicycle.

"What's so funny?" Bobby asked.

"I was thinking about that time you tied my bicycle to the tail of Mr. Blanton's crop duster."

Bobby stopped short in front of the Dip Cone ice cream shop and doubled over with laughter. "I'm not sure who was more surprised, Mr. Blanton or our third-grade class."

Bliss closed her eyes and saw the image as clearly as if she were still that little girl on her first ever Latagnier Elementary field trip. Thanks to Bobby's father, the entire class was invited out to the airstrip to sing the national anthem before the president addressed a collection of local dignitaries and former military men on Veteran's Day. Mr. Tratelli, who'd made the president's acquaintance during the Second World War, was granted the honor of hosting the hour-long stop on the commander in chief's tour of the South.

Just about the time the third graders sang the line about the rockets' red glare, old Mr. Blanton ignored the ban on using the airstrip during the high-profile visit and landed his crop duster within full view of the assembled throng. Newspapers the next day carried a photograph of a stunned president ducking behind a podium, with the mangled remains of a pink Barbie bike surrounded by sparks, its formerly white front tire in flames, in the background.

In the lower left-hand corner of the picture were the host and his wife. While the former Flying Tiger could be seen glaring toward a crowd of innocent-looking schoolchildren, his wife's grin could not be hidden despite the fact that her white-gloved hand partially covered her mouth.

"That was priceless." Bliss watched the light at Martin Street turn yellow, then red, before returning her attention to Bobby. "I'd say it was the Secret Service, though. When that crop duster landed and the sparks started flying, I thought poor Mr. Blanton was going to be shot."

Bobby ducked his head. "Hey, that was nothing compared to what happened when I got home."

"And all because you and Landon told me your daddy could make bicycles fly. Of course I had to dare you to prove it."

"Landon and I never could resist a dare, no matter what the consequences." A strange look came over Bobby's face. Seconds later, he seemed to shake it off. "I should get you inside. I'm sure you're freezing."

He ushered her into the warm interior of the Java Hut, a former feed store now restored as a place for coffee and conversation. Tonight a roaring fire danced in the rock-clad fireplace, the only new addition to the expansive space.

"How about there?" Bobby gestured toward a pair of leather armchairs set facing the fire. With their backs to the room, the seats offered a private place for talking without being overheard. Something about the thought of sitting there with Bobby rattled her.

"Perfect," she said anyway.

Bliss allowed Bobby to help her out of her coat. "It's nice here," she said as she settled into the depths of the soft chair. Except for what looked to be a study group, the place was empty.

"It is, but I liked it better when it was the feed store. Hey, this is progress, I suppose." He rested his hands on the opposite chair and surveyed the room before meeting Bliss's gaze. "So, what can I get you?"

A jolt of high-energy java sounded—and smelled—wonderful. Good sense and expensive medical advice reigned, however. "Do you think they might have some Earl Grey on that long list of teas I saw? I have to confess, without my reading glasses, it all looked like gibberish."

"Yep, I saw it on the list." He pointed to his eye, then winked. "Contacts."

While she watched, Bobby placed their orders at the counter where farmers once ordered seed for the winter. He returned with their drinks and silently sipped at his coffee while Bliss dunked her tea bag in the steaming water. She waited for it to steep, forcing her memories not to cascade backward in time. "How quickly time passes."

"Hmm?"

Bliss looked up sharply as she dug her fingers into the soft leather arm of the chair. "I'm sorry. Did I say that out loud?"

He set his cup down and reached over to rest his hand atop hers a second before removing it. "You okay, Bliss?"

"Of course," she said, hoping Bobby would take that answer without questioning it. "I wonder, though," she continued, "what's been happening with you all these years?"

"Me? Oh, I don't know that there's much to tell. It all turned out pretty much like everyone expected. I took over the family business. Guess that's about it."

She watched him speak, trying to decide if he was hiding something or merely downplaying the more interesting facts in his past. His poker face gave her no clues.

"Well, that might be true, but I suspect there's more to the story, Bobby. Why don't you tell me about Amy?"

He stretched out his legs and rested his booted feet on the edge of the fireplace. When Bliss glanced up, she saw a change in expression. "Amy." He spoke the name as soft as a caress. "The light of my life."

Bliss tucked her feet beneath her and dragged her coat across her legs. "Tell me about her," she urged.

"Amy was—is—an amazing gift from God." He took another sip of coffee, then stared down into the cup as if studying the dark liquid. "Do you know what a gift is, Bliss?"

Their gazes met, and Bliss shook her head. "What do you mean?"

"A gift," he said slowly, "is something you didn't know you wanted until you got it." He paused as if deciding whether to go on. "I didn't know I wanted Amy. Actually, that's not true. I was certain I didn't." He set the cup down with a clatter, then ran his hand through his hair. "I can't believe I said that out loud."

"It's okay."

"No." He gave her a desperate look, then glanced around to see if anyone was near. "I can talk to you, Bliss. I'm not sure why, but I can."

She tried to make light of the serious mood. "Sure you can," she said with a wink. "After all, you didn't tell anyone who put Jell-O in the chemistry teacher's grade book. I certainly owe you."

The slightest hint of a smile touched Bobby's lips. "We all owed you for passing chemistry, Bliss. At least those of us who needed it. But you asked about Amy. . . ."

"You don't have to say anything else. I shouldn't have pried."

"No, I want to tell you." He shifted positions to lean against the arm of the chair. "See, there was a time when I lost touch with the road the Lord put me on. I thought I knew better than He did."

"Been there," Bliss said.

"Not like this, I'm guessing." He frowned. "I want you to understand that I was just a kid. You and Landon were off at school."

When he paused, Bliss said nothing.

"Amy's mother's name was Karen." He paused. "I didn't love her, but she was crazy about me."

Bliss let the statement hang in the air between them, and she reached for her cup of Earl Grey. The warm liquid slid down her throat as she watched the flames dance and listened to the logs crackle.

"But I lost my heart to my daughter as soon as I laid eyes on her."

She looked over and smiled. "And Amy still has your heart."

"Yeah, she does." He let out a long breath. "Karen was a makeup artist on the West Texas shoot. I was a kid, but she wasn't. That doesn't excuse what happened. There's no excuse, really."

Another pause. It was Bliss's turn to rest her hand on his. "It's all in the past."

"Yeah," he said slowly, "it is. I found out about Amy when Karen called my grandpa and told him she had just given birth to his great-granddaughter. By then I was back in college working at A&M on an aviation engineering degree. I met Karen and my daughter on the tarmac of the Latagnier Airstrip three days later. We went straight to the justice of the peace and got married. That's how I spent my twentieth birthday. The next day, I withdrew from A&M and went to work for my father. After all," he said with a grin, "I had a family to support."

"But you were twenty."

"Yeah." He shrugged. "It seemed pretty old at the time."

Bliss tried to take this in. Shy, quiet Bobby a husband and father while she and Landon languished in college?

"Why didn't I know any of this?"

Bobby shrugged. "We'd all begun to lose track of one another by then. Landon came in and stood up for me as best man. We talked about calling you, but what would I have said? Back then I was still in. . ."

He'd almost said it. Almost told Bliss he'd been so in love with her that he couldn't even be man enough to find any feelings for his new wife. Couldn't call to tell his dear friend he was married or had a daughter.

Bob sighed and reached for the coffee cup. All these years and he'd managed to hide it. Why was he running his mouth now? Best bring this conversation to a close before he made a complete fool of himself.

"Anyway," he said, "the short version is that I learned to love her and we had a good life together."

Bliss looked away. "I'm glad."

She wouldn't ask anything further; he knew this. Still, he'd told this much of the story. Might as well tell the rest.

"Then she died." He waved away Bliss's comment. "See, she knew she was dying when she called Grandpa Tratelli. She didn't really want to be married to me; she wanted a home for our daughter. I'll never really know if she loved me or not. Guess that's what I deserve."

Bob set his feet on the floor and stood. "I'm sorry, Bliss, but I need to go. Can I walk you home?"

Again, he knew she wouldn't ask, wouldn't complain at the half-full cup of Earl Grey on the table between them. He helped her into her coat. Then, as they stepped out into the cold, he reached for her hand.

They walked the four blocks in silence again, not because he had nothing to say, but because he had too much to say. It was simpler not to speak at all.

At the door, Bliss stabbed at the lock several times. "Guess I need to look into some contacts," she said.

"Guess so," Bob said as he took the keys from her and opened the door.

Bob looked down into her eyes, got lost in them, and swallowed hard. She'd been pretty as a girl, even prettier as a young woman. But tonight in the café, with the firelight in her hair and the gentle signs of age on her face, well, he'd never seen Bliss look so lovely.

Bliss reached for the keys, and he dropped them into her palm, then wrapped his hand around hers. Her fingers were warm in his.

Somehow he found himself leaning down, moving toward those eyes. Those lips. Was it his imagination, or did she lift onto her toes to inch upward?

A horn honked, and Bliss jumped backward, slamming against the door. The keys went flying, and Bob nearly lost his balance.

"Evening, Miss Emmeline," Bliss called to the town's grande dame and eldest citizen.

"You two behaving yourselves?" the woman called from her cherry red sedan.

"Yes, ma'am," Bobby answered, "we're trying to."

"Well, all right then," the elderly woman responded. "Bliss, tell your mama I'll be seeing her at the quilt guild." With that, she sped off down Main.

Retrieving the keys, Bob stuck them into the lock to keep

from coming too close to Bliss. He couldn't do that. Not until he got a handle on whatever insanity had possessed him.

"Bobby," she whispered, and he placed his forefinger against her lips.

"Good night, Bliss. Go inside now."

Something that looked like disappointment crossed her face, then quickly disappeared. She nodded and turned. Bob watched Bliss disappear inside, watched the door close and the light go on.

With nothing left to do but leave, Bob trudged down the steps toward his truck. "What's wrong with you?" he whispered. "You told her to go inside. What did you expect?"

"Bobby, wait."

Bob looked over his shoulder to see Bliss in the doorway. "What?"

"Come here."

"Why?"

She affected an exasperated look. "I may live downtown, but I do have neighbors. Do you want me to give them something to talk about, or are you going to come over here?"

Bob chuckled despite himself. What in the world was this woman up to?

He slammed the truck door and hit the alarm, then trotted toward the door of the Cake Bake. "Okay," he said, "I'm here."

Bliss smiled. "You didn't have to lock your truck. This *is* Latagnier, after all."

Standing on the porch felt awkward, but going inside wasn't an option. "What did you want to tell me?" he finally asked.

"That I think you're wrong about Karen."

"Look, Bliss, I really don't want to talk about—"

"You're a good man, Bobby Tratelli. If I can see it, I know Karen could. If she didn't think that, why would she have bothered to look for you after she had the baby?"

Bliss reached up on tiptoe to wrap her arms around his neck. For a moment longer, the years were held at bay. Then it was time to leave.

seven

Bob pulled his truck to a stop in front of the Tratelli Aviation offices and shifted into park. Beyond the nondescript building, the Latagnier Airstrip's wind sock showed a stiff north breeze. The flags flying to the right of the front doors confirmed this.

His thoughts shifted back to the topic that had been running through his mind all night, the one that kept him from sleeping, the fear that finally caused him to drag out of bed for a five-mile run well before daylight.

That fear was that he might be falling in love with Bliss Denison all over again. The same Bliss who'd made it clear decades ago that they'd never be more than friends.

Bliss was back in Latagnier and, sadly, back in his heart. Something must be done. While he couldn't force her out of town, he could force her out of his mind. . .eventually.

He'd have to start by firing her mother. Of course, given the luck he'd had with office help, it shouldn't take long to find a reason to let the older woman go.

With renewed resolve, Bob climbed out of the truck and snagged his briefcase. By the time he'd pushed through the doors of Tratelli Aviation, he'd almost perfected his good-bye speech to Bliss's mother.

To his surprise, however, the perpetually messy desk where he expected to find Mrs. Denison was wiped clean. No piles of paper, only neat trays with IN and OUT labels met his gaze. He inhaled deeply of the scent of fresh coffee.

"Oh, there you are." Mrs. Denison rounded the corner dressed in a dark blue suit that made her look more like a flight attendant than his assistant.

"Good morning," he said slowly.

"What's wrong?" She looked down at her outfit and back at him. "Is there something wrong with what I'm wearing?"

"What? Wrong? Oh no," he said. "It's just that we're a bit more casual here." Bob glanced down at his own khakis and golf shirt. "But suit yourself. You look lovely."

"Why thank you, Bobby." She paused to shake her head. "I mean, Mr. Tratelli."

"Bob's fine. Or Bobby, if you prefer," he said as he headed for his office.

A few minutes later, the door opened and Bliss's mother slipped in. Resting against her hip was a tray holding an ancient coffeepot, a mug, cream, sugar, and the morning paper. Upon closer inspection, he noticed a granola bar, an apple, and a stack of notes.

A glance at the clock told him the time was twenty-five minutes to eight. Five minutes into the workday, and he had hot coffee and a person on the other side of the intercom who could actually pronounce his name.

Life was getting better by the minute. Except for the fact that he had to find a way to fire her before the end of the day.

Bob watched his newest temp set the tray on the corner of his desk, then arrange the breakfast in front of him. He let her fuss over the placement of the items while he reached for the papers. "What are these?"

"Wedding planners." Mrs. Denison straightened and clasped her hands together. "I know I could have e-mailed them to you, but personally I like to have something in front of me to jot notes on. That's why I gave each planner a separate sheet."

Bob flipped through the pages, noting that not only had Bliss's mother researched planners in the New Orleans area, but she'd also found a few in the much closer cities of Lafayette and New Iberia. In all, there were close to three dozen possibilities for salvaging Amy's wedding.

"Thank you." Bob shook his head. "You've only been on the clock a few minutes, and you've already accomplished more than the other temps combined."

Mrs. Denison flushed with the compliment. "I'm glad you're pleased. I can call them, of course, but I thought you might want to do the calling yourself."

"Yes, I prefer to handle this myself." He gave her a sideways look. "How did you know I was about to ask for the wedding planner information?"

"I said to myself, 'What's the first thing that man's going to want to get done this morning?' After hearing you talk about your girl last night, I knew exactly what would be on your mind."

Bob didn't correct her. Better she not know what had actually been on his mind.

"Is there anything else you need right now?" she continued. "If not, I'm going to see if I can make heads or tails of the mess I found in the files. Would you believe some fool's taken every piece of mail that came through since Yvonne left and filed it under *M* for mail?"

Bob felt his brows raise as he shook his head. "No, that's fine. You go right ahead. I've got plenty to do."

Bliss's mother left, shaking her head and muttering something under her breath about careless young people and taking time to do things right.

"Thank You, Lord," he whispered as he poured a cup of coffee and doused it with cream, then sprinkled sugar in. "You did provide. I'm sorry I doubted." He sighed. "I guess I can't fire her, can I?"

He knew the answer. If only he could figure out a permanent solution to the feelings he feared were growing for Bliss.

The temporary solution was distraction, easily found by concentrating on the disaster of the day: Amy's wedding. He started with the first planner on the stack, an outfit based in New Orleans.

"Hello, Wedding Wonders," the friendly female voice said.

"Yes, my daughter's getting married," Bob said. "She's out of the country right now, so I'm on my own here."

The person on the other end of the line chuckled. "I'm sure we can help. How many people will be invited?"

"Around twelve hundred."

There was a long pause. "Did you say twelve hundred guests?"

It was hard to miss the glee in the woman's tone. "I did," he responded.

"If you'll hold on a second, I'll crunch some numbers and grab my calendar." Two minutes of smooth jazz later, the woman was back. "All right, now, let's talk details. When's the big day?"

"The last Saturday in March," he said as he reached for his pen.

"Wonderful. That gives us thirteen months to—"

"No, ma'am," Bob said. "That's this March."

"What?" The woman's tone seemed a bit icy. "Next month?"

Bob leaned back in his chair and tossed the pen back onto the desk. "Yes."

"Any chance of moving that date back a bit? Say sometime this summer? With four months' notice, I can create magic."

"Not a chance," Bob said.

"Sorry," she said, "but we can't help you."

He reached for the slip with Wedding Wonders written across the top and crumpled it. The next eight calls brought the same response. On the ninth try, he changed his tactics.

"So," he said casually to the proprietor of Weddings by Latrice, "how much will it cost to give my daughter the wedding of her dreams a month from now?"

Click.

"All right." Bob tossed another slip into the trash. "So that didn't work."

He thumbed through the remaining slips of paper and found three locations in Lafayette and two in New Iberia. Five choices remaining out of several dozen.

"This is not looking good, Lord. Could You send me some help—and fast?"

The intercom buzzed. "Excuse me, Mr. Tratelli. Yvonne is on line one."

His hopes rose. Never could he remember the Lord answering his prayers so quickly. "Thank you, Mrs. Denison." Bob reached for the phone and pressed the blinking light. "Yvonne, it's great to hear from you. Are you enjoying your vacation?"

"I'm having a fine time, but there's just one *tiny* problem I had to call and tell you about."

At the word *problem*, Bob's heart sank. "What's wrong, Yvonne?"

"Well, it's the funniest thing. We were just sitting down to breakfast this morning, and Jack said, 'Isn't it a shame we have to leave soon?' and I said, 'Well, yes, I suppose it is.'" She paused. "I never expected he would *do* something about it."

Bob rose and walked to the window in time to see a Tratelli Aviation Embraer 110 take off on the eastbound runway. "Do something? Something like what?"

"He, well. . . Jack bought me an early anniversary gift. How was I going to tell him no?"

"Tell him no about what, Yvonne?"

"Are you sitting down?"

He sank into his chair. "I am now."

❧

Bliss closed her eyes and lifted her face toward the warmth of the February sun, her bare feet just inches from the black water of Bayou Nouvelle. The trickle of slow-moving currents combined with the call of a spoonbill and the sharp staccato rap of a distant woodpecker to form an unforgettable symphony.

This had been the soundtrack of her childhood, the music to which most of her youthful memories had been set. Today it formed a hymn of praise to the Creator, a song of thanks for all that was good in Bliss's world.

Yesterday's chill had given way to this morning's warm spell, typical for weather in southern Louisiana. With her walking shoes cast off and her hooded sweatshirt forming the pillow under her head, Bliss laced her fingers together and let out a long, satisfied breath.

The beauty of the moment was only enhanced by the fact that she could do this all day. She could actually lie in the sun and do nothing.

Do nothing—a concept so foreign to her this time last year that she would have told anyone who would listen that it was impossible. No one could just sit. Just be.

The partial truth in that was that no one in her old world, the world of the Bentley and its bustling kitchens and nonstop demands, could imagine lying beside a bayou on a Thursday morning in the middle of nowhere obeying nothing but the requirement that the next breath must be taken.

Bliss smiled, then counted the movement as her first conscious effort in a full three minutes. She'd come a long way since the first time she slipped off to her old hiding place at Bayou Nouvelle. She'd done it to appease Mama. Mama who worried too much. Mama who shadowed Bliss like a hawk in those first weeks back in Latagnier.

Something about Bliss's trips to the bayou made Mama worry less. Bliss could now admit it was because *she* worried less. Now, instead of allowing the what-ifs and the why-mes to pile atop her shoulders, Bliss climbed into her car and drove to the bayou to forget her worries beside the chocolate waters of the Nouvelle.

In place of her worries, a fullness that could only come from the Lord filled her heart. She called the spot where she now lay the Lazarus place: the place where her heart had been recalled from the dead.

A place where her life had not just been saved but had been resurrected.

Some would argue and say the emergency room at Austin's Brackenridge Hospital was owed that honor. Or perhaps the kind EMT who prayed with her in the ambulance while keeping her alive. In the physical sense, both would be right.

But this place, this secluded patch of soft ground, had kept her alive even after medical intervention had been exhausted. It was the place she went to remember why she wanted to live. And to learn all over again how to live.

Bliss hated to think about the dark days after the accident, but sometimes she allowed the thoughts to return. The contrast between then and now served as a reminder of who and what mattered. It also kept her mindful of just Who remained in charge.

There were no neat solutions, no pat answers to difficult questions, and there certainly were no guarantees that the tiny time bomb the doctors had found wouldn't be the end of her despite their best guesses to the contrary. This, Bliss now knew, was nothing she could change by fretting. It was the Lord's to fix.

Or not to fix.

Even when she'd believed in her heart of hearts that she was completely in charge of her life, she hadn't really been. Somehow the knowledge that the sure and steady hands of the Lord held the future, and not her own trembling fingers, made the uncertainty all right.

Bliss exhaled again and studied the oranges and yellows that decorated the backs of her eyelids. The earthy scent of Louisiana mud floated past on a soft breeze. An egret called, and the pines swished in response.

Just another Thursday morning in paradise.

The snap of a twig brought her eyes wide open. There, on a limb not far from her, was the egret. Swishing about in a flurry of lacy white feathers, the long-legged creature aimed its orange beak in her direction, then showed its profile and the odd green smudge at the eyes that characterized the gangly swamp birds. The roar of an airplane sent the bird airborne, and Bliss watched it cross the bayou and disappear.

She tracked the plane across the sky until it, too, was gone. The logo on the jet had been hard to miss.

Tratelli Aviation.

What a strange tangle of emotions thoughts of Bobby Tratelli brought. Bliss sighed. There were precious few old friends in her life, and welcoming a new one back should not have such mixed feelings attached to it.

Bliss rose and slid into her shoes, then gathered her sweatshirt up and tied it around her waist. Testing the soundness of her knee, she was surprised to feel not even a twinge. After last night's stroll, she figured to be paying for the exertion today.

Looking to the left, she could almost make out the hood of her car peeking through the underbrush. She hadn't dared park so far away that she couldn't easily return. Now she turned to the right. From her childhood memories, she knew there was a clearly defined path along the bayou. It ran behind the Trahan place, wound past the schoolhouse, and ended just beyond the old church.

It had been ages since Bliss followed that path. Perhaps today was the day to do just that.

eight

Bob stared at the pieces of paper before him. He'd started with more than thirty wedding planners to contact. Now there were only five.

Then there was the matter of contacting Amy. He hadn't talked to her since Tuesday. Thankfully, that conversation hadn't been marred by the knowledge that her wedding plans had fallen apart. The next one would, however, unless he managed to fix the problem today.

She'd be home Sunday evening, so even if he managed to keep the topic of the wedding out of the conversation—which was doubtful at best—there'd be no missing the lack of a wedding planner come Monday morning. "This is a mess," he whispered. "A huge mess."

Bob sighed and pushed away from his desk. So much for depending on Yvonne to help. Not that he could fault her for leaving him.

"Who wouldn't be thrilled with a condo on the beach in Waikiki with a balcony overlooking Diamond Head?" he said as he stood and stretched the kinks out of his neck.

Not that Hawaii was his cup of tea. Too many people and you couldn't even see the stars for all the lights in Honolulu. Now, put him on a horse somewhere with lots of land—that would be a vacation.

Bob rolled his shoulders and felt the stiffness give a bit. He should call Amy. She needed to know. He leaned over and reached for the phone, then set it back down and sank onto the chair again.

"I can't let her down," he said softly. "I just can't. There are still five left. Surely one of them will take on the impossible."

He divided the stacks by city and tackled the two in New Iberia first. The first one hung up on him when he gave them the date, and the second tried to offer him half price for moving the wedding from Latagnier to a casino docked near Lake Charles. He politely declined.

Bob tossed both slips of paper into the trash, then placed the last three pages in front of him. Three names, three more chances to make things right.

He closed his eyes and prayed, then reached for the one in the middle: Divine Occasions. A recording told him to leave a message, so he did. The second one, a place called Exquisite Events, thought he was playing a practical joke on them, while the third, Acadian Wedding Planners, followed in the grand tradition of hanging up when he stated the urgency of the matter.

"I'm in a fine fix now, Lord," he said softly. "The only place that hasn't turned me down is this one, and I'm sure it's a matter of time before they do."

"Now, you don't know that." Mrs. Denison stood in the doorway, her fingers over her mouth. "I'm sorry, I didn't mean to overhear. I saw the light go out on the phone and thought it would be a good time to deliver the mail."

"Yes, of course, come on in."

Bob walked over to the window and tried to make sense of the mess. He had one chance left to make Amy's wedding the one she deserved. What were the odds that Divine Occasions would take on the project?

"So," Bliss's mother said lightly, "did you have a chance to call the. . . Oh, I see you did."

He turned around to see her studying the wastebasket, now overflowing with crumpled pages. "It seems as though the consensus is that my timeline's a bit too tight for them." When she looked confused, he clarified. "Nowadays a wedding takes more than a month to pull off. I had no idea."

"Well, in my day it surely didn't." She smiled. "Why, my dear husband, rest his soul, and I didn't have all this fuss. He took a notion to ask me to marry him, and I said yes. Mama gathered flowers from the garden, and my papa drove me to New Iberia to buy a pretty new dress. We were married in my grandparents' front parlor and had cake and coffee afterward right there in the dining room." She paused as if remembering the day. " 'Course we were more concerned with making our way in the world than the young folks nowadays. We couldn't have afforded anything grand. Your Amy, now she's already got her life arranged. It wasn't like that for me. I had my sights set on a home and babies."

"She does have her life arranged, doesn't she?"

"Seems to."

Bob paused to think on that, and his hopes soared. Amy was a smart young woman. Surely she would see the wisdom in a small wedding.

"You know, Mrs. Denison, I have to wonder if yours wasn't the better way." He paused to convince himself further. "I'll bet Amy would be just as happy with a small gathering and just a few friends and family."

"Oh, I don't know. She might. Although what bride wouldn't want to feel like a princess on her big day?" Bliss's mother giggled. "And since when does a member of the Breaux family have a small wedding?"

He sighed. Mrs. Denison certainly spoke the truth. Even limiting the guest list to first cousins would make the numbers bulge well past what any local restaurant would hold.

"I suppose you're right."

"About what?" She paused. "Oh, now don't let me be putting ideas into your head. This isn't my wedding or yours. It's Amy's. If I were you, I'd find out what Amy wants and stick to that."

He met her gaze. "But how am I going to do that? To find out, I'd have to tell her there's a problem."

"You haven't done that yet?" She planted her hands on her hips. "Bobby Tratelli, you have to tell her." The moment the words were out, she looked as if she wanted to reel them back in. "I'm sorry. That was none of my business and certainly not something an employee—even a temporary one—should be saying."

"Uh, Mrs. Denison? About your employment."

She eyed him suspiciously. "What about it?"

He gestured to the chair on the opposite side of the desk. "Sit down. There's something I'd like to discuss with you."

"If it's the coffeepot, that fancy new one's not broken. I just set it under the sink, but I can get it out and use it again if you'd like. It's just that I prefer the percolator. Gives a much better cup of coffee in my—"

Bob sank down in his chair and held his hands up to silence her. "No, it's not the coffee. In fact, the cup I had this morning's the best I've ever tasted." He grinned. "Although if you were to tell my mama that, I'd have to deny it."

"I'm pleased that you liked it. The trick is to mix just the right amount of chicory with the coffee. Once you get that figured out, the rest is easy." She giggled. "And if it makes you feel any better, your mama was the one who showed me how to make it."

They shared a laugh; then Bob grew serious. "Mrs. Denison, something's happened to change the situation here at Tratelli Aviation."

"Oh?" She fumbled with the brass buttons on her sleeve. "I hope it's nothing serious. I know you've got a lot on your mind what with Amy's wedding and all. Is it something I might be able to help with?"

He exhaled slowly. "Yes, I believe it might be."

Mrs. Denison waited patiently while Bob chose his words.

And, to her credit, she waited in silence. Bob had hired and fired a number of people in his day, and he'd learned that the good ones—the employees who stuck around and earned their keep—were the ones who could wait in silence.

"As you know, Yvonne phoned this morning from Hawaii." When she nodded, he continued. "Seems as though she won't be returning to her job here."

"Oh?" She shifted positions and affected an innocent look. "What will you do?"

Something in her manner gave Bob the impression that Mrs. Denison already knew there was an opening at Tratelli Aviation for an executive assistant. He also suspected Yvonne told her before she worked up the courage to tell him.

"What will I do?" He leaned forward, resting his elbows on the desk as he steepled his hands. "What I thought I would do is offer the job to you. If you'd like it, that is."

Her eyes twinkled. "Well," she said slowly, "my husband, rest his soul, always told me not to buy the horse till you'd inspected its teeth."

"I'm sorry?"

Mrs. Denison sat a little straighter and gave him a direct look. "I'm going to need to know just what you'd be paying me. And then there's the benefits package. There is one, isn't there?"

He leaned back, and the chair squeaked loudly. "Of course."

"What about vacation?"

"Two weeks for the first three years, then three. After five years, you'll be eligible for a month."

She shook her head. "That won't do. I'll need four to start. I don't 'spect I'll need to go any higher than that, so don't worry. We'll just keep it at four from now on out."

Bob suppressed a smile. "Anything else?"

His assistant looked past him to the window. "Those planes of yours—they ever take people?"

"We've got a fleet of corporate jets for hire. Those carry people." He studied her with curiosity. "Why?"

"My husband's got a brother—a stepbrother, actually, but he never thought of him as anything other than blood kin—and he's over in Florida. Moved in with his son and daughter-in-law two summers ago. Greg—that's his name—keeps asking me to bring Bliss down there to visit." She leaned forward. "You figure my daughter and I might catch a ride down to Tampa on one of those planes? During my vacation time, of course."

Bob pretended to consider it. "I think we might be able to work something out."

She sat back. "I'm not hearing anything definite in that statement."

"All right. Yes, once a year I will okay a flight to Tampa for you and Bliss." He paused. "The jets generally hold eight, some of them twelve. Feel free to fill those empty seats."

Her poker face slipped. "You serious?"

"I'm serious." He rose and offered her his hand. "What do you say, Mrs. Denison? Will you accept the job as my assistant?"

"Don't you want to see my work history? Maybe get some recommendations? 'Course I worked for my father-in-law— that's Mr. Ben Denison—over at the sawmill until I met my husband, Mr. Ben's younger son. I kept books for him and ran the office until Bliss came along. Once my husband took over for his daddy, Bliss and I started coming to work with him, and before I knew it, I was running that office again. I did that until the mill sold three years ago. It's what he wanted, rest his soul, but I don't believe my husband realized what he was doing when he asked me to part with that job."

"All the more reason to take this one," Bob said gently. "It's yours as long as you want it, and I promise there are no plans to sell the place." He paused. "In fact, I had hoped to pass it on to Amy someday. I don't know if she'll want it, but I pray she does."

"Well, that's a prayer I'll join you in."

"And joining the company? What's your position on that?"

Mrs. Denison studied him a second longer, then nodded and shook on the deal. She climbed to her feet and straightened her sleeves, then headed for the door, her back straight as an arrow.

Pausing at the door, Bliss's mother met his stare. "Mr. Tratelli?"

"Why don't you call me Bob?" He paused. "Or Bobby's fine, too."

"All right. Bobby?" She ducked her head. "Do you realize how old I am?"

"I'm sure I could find out easily," he said. "But I don't think it matters." He paused to offer a smile. "Do you?"

Once again, she fell silent. Her response was to press her finger to her lips and disappear into the lobby. A moment later, her voice came through the intercom. "Your conference call is ready for you on line two."

"Thank you, Mrs. Denison." Bob paused before reaching for the phone. "Thank You, Lord, for arranging this. I'm not sure what You're up to, but I do pray You will keep me posted so I can do my part."

An hour later, he hung up from the call and read over his notes, adding to them where he felt more information was needed. When he was done, he stuffed the information into the folder and set it aside.

A check of his watch revealed it was nearly ten thirty. He buzzed the front desk. "Mrs. Denison, has the wedding planner in Lafayette returned my call?"

"No, sir," she quickly responded. "Do you want me to get them on the line?"

"Yes, please," he answered. "It's Divine Occasions on Ambassador Caffery."

A few minutes later, she appeared at the door. "I'm sorry, boss. I had to leave a message."

He nodded. "That's odd, don't you think?"

"I don't know," Mrs. Denison said. "Maybe they're just busy."

"Maybe." He thought a moment. "What does my calendar look like for the rest of the day?"

"I'll check." She returned with the leather-bound planner. "Chamber of commerce luncheon at noon, tux fitting at three, and a meeting with your broker at five." Her gaze lifted to meet his. "That's it."

"Cancel the fitting and reschedule the meeting with my broker for Tuesday." He reached for his keys.

"Are you leaving?"

"I can't just sit around waiting for the wedding planner to call me back. I'm going to drive over to Lafayette and pay them a visit. They can't ignore me if I'm standing in front of them." He paused to search her face, and she seemed troubled. "What? Do you think it's a bad idea?"

"Well, not completely," she said slowly. "Do you know what Amy's plans were for the wedding?"

"They should be in the e-mails she sent me."

Mrs. Denison nodded. "Hold on a second, and I'll print them off." In no time, she returned with a blue file folder. She thrust it toward him. "Something blue," she said with a giggle.

"What?"

"You know," she said, "something old, something new, something borrowed, something *blue*."

"Oh, sure, got it." He smiled. "So this has everything I need?"

Her nod was without enthusiasm. "What? You're not telling me something. What is it?"

"Well, it's just that I wonder whether you should go alone."

She paused. "What I mean is, sending a man by himself into a wedding planner's offices is sort of like sending a woman into Sears to buy power tools. She might have a list, but will she really know what she's looking at?"

"Hmm, I see your point." He snagged his jacket. "That's easily fixed. I'll swing by and fetch Neecie. She'll know what she's looking at."

"Sure," Mrs. Denison said. Once again, her lack of enthusiasm was evident in her expression.

Bob paused at the door. "What?"

Mrs. Denison shrugged. "Oh, I was just wondering if Neecie would be willing to close up shop a second day to go running off to Lafayette. It's so far."

"Nah, it's less than an hour. Besides, she and I go way back. I'm sure she'd be glad to help out an old friend." Bob loped out of the office and climbed into the truck with a light heart. Tonight when Amy called, he'd have something positive to tell her. That alone made him smile.

Sure, he'd lost Yvonne to blue Hawaii—and he'd miss her terribly—but in the process, the Lord had brought Mrs. Denison to fill her absence. The truck rolled over the ruts on the parish road, then fishtailed onto the empty highway. Ten minutes later, he pulled to a stop in front of Wedding Belles and bounded to the door.

It was locked.

"Neecie," Bob called as he pounded on the door. "Open up! It's me, Bob."

Shielding his eyes with his hand, Bob peered inside the depths of the darkened store. *Please, Lord, Mrs. Denison's right. I can't do this on my own. Please provide someone. Anyone.*

He resumed his pounding. "Neecie, come on," Bob finally said. "I know you're in there. You have to be. It's Thursday. You can't be gone."

"But she is."

Bob whirled around to see Bliss standing on the sidewalk. From the running shoes, sweatpants, and ponytail, he deduced she'd been to the gym. She tossed her cell phone into a small black purse and fished out a key on a large round ring.

"Where is she?"

Bliss shrugged and stabbed the key toward the lock. "No idea, but I'm beginning to get worried about her." Several attempts later, Bob walked over and took the key from Bliss, fitting it into the lock on the first try.

"I know," Bliss said as she accepted the key from him. "I've got an appointment for contacts next Tuesday."

Any other time, he would have made a joke, possibly made light of the fact that she'd need to carry around her reading glasses until then. This, however was a desperate moment, and he was a man with little time to spare. Since the Lord didn't see fit to bring Neecie back in time to go with him to Lafayette, He must have intended for Bliss to accompany him.

In light of the tangle of feelings Bob still hadn't unraveled, Bliss was not his first choice. Obviously he and the Lord saw things differently.

Bob took in the woman's appearance and shook his head. "Bliss, I'm in a hurry here. Get out of those clothes and climb into the truck."

nine

"Excuse me?" Bliss gave the lunatic the look he deserved and pressed past him to step inside. She would've slammed the door in his face, but for a big guy, he moved awfully fast.

In more ways than one, if his pickup line was to be believed. *Pickup line.* Bliss groaned at the pun and kept walking.

"Wait, what? What did I say?"

"Get out of my clothes and get into your truck?" She pressed her forefinger into his chest. "Since when does that line work, buddy? Surely not with this girl."

His face went white, and he began waving his hands frantically. "Oh no, Bliss, that's not what I meant."

Hands on her hips, Bliss stared him down. "Then what *did* you mean?"

"I just meant those clothes have got to go."

She left him standing beside the counter. "Go home, Bobby. I'll tell Neecie to call you when she gets in."

"I don't have time to wait for her." Heavy footsteps echoed behind her. "I need you, Bliss, and I need you now."

Bliss stopped short and whirled around, nearly slamming into his chest. As she backed up two paces, she made the odd observation that he smelled quite nice.

Bobby shook his head. "Look, I'm sorry. I just meant that I can't take you dressed like that."

"Like what?"

"Like that." He pointed to her ponytail, then allowed his gaze to slide past her purple LSU Tigers T-shirt to land on the sidewalk.

She looked down at the grass stains on her shoes and the

84

gray sweatshirt wrapped around her midsection. He did have a point. Still. . . "Who said I was going anywhere with you?"

"Bliss, you have every right to tell me no. I mean, I haven't exactly been saying all the right things, and we did almost kiss each other yesterday, which would have been a huge disaster."

A huge disaster? Ouch. She bit her lip to keep from responding.

Bobby started pacing. "And you're the *last* woman I want to ride to Lafayette with."

Ouch again.

"I'd much rather take someone like Neecie who doesn't make my brain feel like scrambled eggs."

Scrambled eggs? That might just redeem the last comment. And the ones before that.

If she could decide exactly what he meant by it.

"How am I doing here, Bliss?" Bobby sighed and stopped pacing to turn and face her. "Look, I'm not good at this. I'm just a dad trying to do the right thing for his daughter."

Bliss leaned against the wall and crossed her arms in front of her. "I'm still not clear on what the right thing is, Bobby. How is dragging me to Lafayette in a party dress going to help your daughter?"

"It doesn't have to be a party dress. Just not something so. . ."

Her raised eyebrow stopped his words. "So?"

"Please?" Bobby met her stare. "All I'm asking is for you to ride with me to Lafayette to check out the only wedding planner in three parishes who hasn't hung up on me."

"Why do I need to come? Can't you do this yourself?"

"I thought of that." He paused. "Your mother said it would be like sending a woman to Sears to buy tools."

Bliss tried to keep her expression neutral. "Well, I can see your point, but this is my day off. I was planning to—"

"Please?"

So much emotion in one little word. Still, it wasn't the word but rather his eyes that proved to be her undoing. Despite all the stupid things he said while trying to be brilliant and persuasive, his eyes sent her scurrying upstairs.

"Make a pot of coffee for the road, okay?" She paused midway up the steps. "You do know how to make coffee, don't you?"

She came downstairs twenty minutes later, expecting to smell coffee perking. Instead, she saw Bobby sitting at her table reading the morning's edition of the Latagnier paper and sipping from a brown paper cup with the words JAVA HUT emblazoned in black beside a gold fleur-de-lis.

He smiled when he saw her, then gestured to a matching cup sitting on the counter. "And you didn't think I knew how to make coffee."

Bliss shook her head. "Let's get this mission started, Bobby, before I change my mind."

"Yes, ma'am." He punctuated the statement with a crisp salute before snagging his coffee cup and trotting behind her out to the sidewalk.

Retrieving her keys, Bliss aimed them at the lock on her shop door, then paused to pull her reading glasses from her purse. Bobby chuckled and headed for the truck to open the door for her.

"So, where are we going again?" Bliss asked as Bobby backed the truck out onto Main and headed north.

"Lafayette." He pointed to a slip of paper folded in half and sitting on the console between them. "A place called Divine Occasions."

"That's a nice name." Bliss retrieved the paper and recognized her mother's handwriting. "Hey, I know where this is. Mama and I checked them out when I was thinking of opening my cake shop. As I recall, the elderly ladies who ran the place were very helpful in giving me advice."

"Good, then you can help me find them." He paused to smile. "And then you can translate."

"Translate?" Bliss watched as he turned just past Latagnier Elementary and headed for the interstate. "As I recall, they spoke perfect English."

Bobby accelerated onto the highway before glancing her way. "Maybe so, but it's already been proven that I don't speak female."

"You've got a point."

"Hey," he said a few minutes later, "thanks for coming with me." He gave Bliss a sideways look. "Honestly, I'm terrified I'm going to mess this up for Amy."

Bliss's heart lurched. How sweet was this? "I won't let you do that, Bobby."

True relief crossed his face. "I appreciate this more than you know," he said slowly. "More than I can say." He paused. "But then, we've already established that I don't speak female."

They shared a laugh, then fell into a companionable silence.

"Hey," he said a few minutes later.

Bliss shifted in the seat to face him. "Yeah?"

His gaze swept over her. "You look nice," he said. "Really nice."

"Thank you."

"I appreciate you doing this. Coming with me, I mean."

"So you said." She smiled. "Really, I've done everything today that I planned. Well, except that book I was going to read. Haven't gotten to that yet."

"Well now," he said with a wink. "I guess I should step on it so you can get back quickly. Wouldn't want you to miss reading your book."

Bliss's eyes narrowed. "Yeah, right. How about you concentrate on being careful instead of fast? I'm kind of over car wrecks."

"What does that mean?" He signaled to change lanes, then shot her a look. "I've never been in a wreck in my life."

"Well," she said slowly, "you're the lucky one then."

Leaning back against the leather seat, Bliss closed her eyes. She knew Bobby was probably looking for an explanation, but the walk she'd taken combined with the hot shower had her relaxed and feeling as limp as. . .

"Bliss?" The word floated softly toward her through cotton-thick clouds. "Bliss?"

Her eyes flew open. Where was she? Heart pounding, Bliss leaned forward only to be snapped back by some sort of restraint.

"Hey there, slow down, darlin'. Let me get the seat belt for you."

Bobby. The truck. A gas station. Beyond that, a freeway.

Slowly these things began to make sense. She was accompanying him somewhere.

Bliss took a deep breath to slow her racing heart, then let it out as Bobby leaned toward her and unsnapped the seat belt. When she met his gaze, he grinned.

"What?" She swiped at her mouth with the back of her hand lest she'd been drooling.

"You talk in your sleep." He opened the door and climbed out, then closed the door behind him.

Bliss watched him slide his credit card, then pump the gas. When he returned, she was ready with a swift response.

"I do not."

Bobby started the truck. "You don't what?"

"I don't talk in my sleep." She buckled her seat belt.

"Bliss," he said slowly, "if you're asleep, how would you know?"

That question alone silenced her for the rest of the short trip into Lafayette. The navigation system on the truck led them directly to Kaliste Saloom Road and Ambassador Caffery, then into the parking lot of a shopping center.

"What's the name of this place again?" Bobby asked.

"Divine Occasions," Bliss said. She pointed to the far end

of the center. "Best as I can remember, it was down there. See the tire center? The place should be just across from it."

Bobby nodded and pointed the truck in that direction. "There. I see it."

He drove past a card shop, two restaurants, and a place that sold Christmas decorations year round to pull the truck to a stop in front of Divine Occasions. Or, at least the place where Divine Occasions used to be.

Bobby sank back in the seat, eyes closed. "This is awful."

"Wait a second," Bliss said. "There's a note on the door. Let me go see what it says."

While the showroom was empty, the note on the door left hope the store might still be in operation. "It says they've moved."

His eyes opened. "Are you sure?"

"I think so." Bliss rifled through her purse until she found a pen and last Tuesday's receipt from the market. "Just a second, and I'll get you the new location." She jogged back up to the door and wrote down an address. "Got it."

She climbed into the truck and handed Bobby the paper, then buckled her seat belt while he programmed in the new address. A moment later, a mechanical voice told them which direction to turn to leave the parking lot.

"I know I keep saying this, Bliss, but I just can't mess up this wedding." His face showed the desperation he must feel. "Amy's all I've got, and I can't let her down."

Bliss rested her hand on his arm. "Look, I think you're putting way too much pressure on yourself. If Amy were worried about you messing anything up, I doubt she would be so casual about the whole thing."

He gave her a sideways look before braking at a red light. "What do you mean?"

"I mean that I'm wondering why she hasn't been pestering you about this."

Bobby seemed to think about this for a moment. "Well, she's been busy. The first two weeks, she was negotiating that new contract with the British cargo company. Did a good job of it, too." He paused to smile. "I talked to her when that was complete."

"When was that?"

"Couple of days ago." He shrugged. "Why?"

"Did she ask about the wedding?"

"Only in passing." Bobby paused. "She asked how it was going. At the time, I thought it was going just fine."

"Did she press you for details?" Bliss's eyes narrowed. "Or did she seem more interested in the contract?"

"You ask interesting questions, Bliss. Let me think a minute. Yeah, I guess I'd say the conversation was about the contract. How excited she was to get a better bargain than she went over there for. She was really excited about that."

"I see."

"What?" Bobby's face wore a stricken look. "What are you thinking?"

"Nothing. I'm just asking questions." She removed her hand from his arm and rested it in her lap. "Don't pay any attention to me. I don't even know Amy. For all I know, she's crazy nuts for this guy she's marrying and can't wait to tie the knot."

Bobby took a sharp left turn at the next intersection and pulled into the parking lot of the Lafayette Parish Savings and Loan. As he threw the truck into park, he reached for his cell phone.

Bliss's eyes widened in surprise. "What are you doing, Bobby?"

"One second." He punched a number into the phone, then held it to his ear. "Calling Amy. I need an answer to your question."

ten

"To my question?" Bliss sighed. "Oh no, Bobby, I didn't mean to cause you to worry. Just ignore me. What do I know? I've never been married. I'm the last one you should—"

"Amy, darlin', this is your pop." His gaze met Bliss's across the cab of the truck. "Yeah, I'm still pretty pumped about that contract, too. You're definitely a chip off the old block. I can't wait for you to tell Grandpa."

Pause.

"No, of course I didn't tell him. This is your deal. You get to tell him."

Another pause.

"Yeah, he and Grandma should be back in another week, ten days at the most. You'll be back well before then. Say, I want to talk to you about something else if you have just a minute." Bobby's brows shot up. "Oh, you don't?"

He looked over at Bliss and shrugged. She offered a smile.

"I understand you've got dinner plans and all, but don't you have just a second to talk about your. . . Well, that is, don't you want to know how things are going here?"

Bliss watched the cars passing by, trying to tune out the conversation. Still, it was a bit difficult not to hear a conversation going on less than a foot away.

"Well, all right," Bobby said. "Sure, I'll take care of everything. You just enjoy Paris."

"Everything all right?" Bliss asked when Bobby hung up.

He stared down at the cell phone, then set it back in the center console's storage compartment. "You were right," he said as he slowly turned toward Bliss.

91

"Right about what?"

"She's not interested in the details of the wedding." He shrugged. " 'I trust you, Daddy.' That's what she told me."

"I see."

"Yeah, I think I see, too." He paused a second before shifting into reverse. "I'm just not sure what I'm going to do about this."

Bliss cleared her throat. "I'm not keen on offering any more words of wisdom, but I will say that I think you need to keep doing what you're doing. Keep planning this wedding until she comes back and takes over. When's she coming back, anyway?"

"Another week," he said.

"Same time Yvonne's due back." She smiled. "See, one more week of this, then you can turn it all over to them."

"Nope." He gunned the engine and shot into an empty spot on the heavily traveled road. "Yvonne's not coming back."

"Really?" She sat up a little straighter and tore her eyes from the road ahead. "Why not?"

"Her husband bought her a condo overlooking Diamond Head. She's retiring."

"Wow. Just like that?"

"Guess so." He braked for a light, and she saw him heave a sigh.

"I know you were depending on her to come back. What will you do now?"

He glanced her way. "That's the one good thing about this. Your mother's agreed to hire on permanently."

"She has?" Bliss considered this piece of news and tried to make sense of it. She'd predicted a few scenarios that might take place once Mama went to work at Tratelli Aviation, but any sort of permanent employment was not one of them. "Well, how about that?"

"You sound disappointed."

"No, I'm surprised." She grinned. "And pleased. She's been lost ever since the sawmill sold. I wonder about something, though. Are you sure you know what you're doing? Mama can be, well, a force of nature, on occasion."

His laughter was contagious. "Actually, that's part of her charm. At least so far. The woman sure can negotiate. I'm still trying to figure out how I agreed to her terms."

"Doesn't surprise me. My granddaddy taught her how to bargain. He always said she had a better head for business than my daddy."

"Still, she's got a better vacation plan than I did coming in, and the owner was my father."

Bliss shook her head. "No, don't bother to try to analyze it. Just go along with her. It's better for all of us if you do."

"She does make a fine cup of coffee," he said. "And she can pronounce my name."

"Has that been a problem?"

"The last temp called me Mr. Tarantino." He shook his head. "The one before that put a guy from Japan on hold, then left for lunch."

"Oh no." The gadget on his dash chirped, indicating their destination was near. "There it is." Bliss pointed to the huge gold letters of Divine Occasions that seemed to float across a sign covered in a cloud of white lights.

"Subtle," Bobby said as he parked and turned off the engine. "At least it looks like this one's actually open for business."

He loped to the sidewalk, then once Bliss joined him, set the truck alarm and headed for the door. "Say a prayer, Bliss. This place is my last hope."

Bliss giggled. "You're going to need those prayers."

"Oh?"

She nodded. "Wait until you meet the Broussard sisters."

Bob shook his head. "Who?"

"The Broussard sisters." Bliss gestured toward the front

doors of Divine Occasions. "Isolde and Isabelle." She opened the door and glanced at Bobby over her shoulder. "Just don't say I didn't warn you."

The first thing to hit her upon entering Divine Occasions was the scent of roses, in buckets sorted by color. Such was the volume of business at the humble establishment that only a few dozen blossoms ever remained at the end of the week. Those, she knew, were donated to the nursing home over by Lafayette General.

Purple curtains at the rear of the room opened to reveal a plus-sized woman dressed in stop-sign red from head to toe. Even her cheek color seemed to have been chosen to match the ensemble.

"Well, I do declare. If it isn't that sweet girl who wanted to open the cake shop. Least I think it is. *Comment ça va, cher?*"

Bobby leaned close. "Which one is that?"

Bliss spoke through her smile. "I have no idea." She turned her attention to the shopkeeper. "*Ça va bien.*" She nodded at the senior citizen with the fire-engine red curls. "Yes, it's me. My, but you have a good memory."

"Isolde and me, we're old, hon, but we don't miss much. Who dis man you wit?" She turned her attention to Bobby. "Now ain't you some specimen? You done good, girl," she said to Bliss. "He's a little long in the tooth for me, but Isolde, she don't mind them so old."

"What?" Bliss struggled to catch up to the subject change. "Oh no, Bobby's not my. . . Well, he's the father of the bride."

"Father of the bride?" Isabelle sized up Bobby, then looked over her shoulder. "Isolde! Put down your window decorations and get on out here. We got customers."

A woman in the same outfit with matching red hair stepped through the curtain. In one hand, she held a collection of extension cords. In the other, a pair of scissors.

"*Mais non*, Isabelle," Isolde said. "This one cannot be a

customer. It's that woman with the funny name. The one who wanted to bake cakes." She set the scissors on the counter and gripped the cords to her ample chest. "But who is this?" Isolde leaned across the counter to check Bobby out. "*Merci*, you are *très* handsome."

"Ladies," Bobby said, "I've got a wedding to pull off, and I don't have much time." Neither seemed bothered by this statement, so he continued. "Twelve hundred invitations went out, and as of two weeks ago, four hundred were coming."

Twin sets of painted-on brows rose. "And when is this *soirée*?"

Bobby took a deep breath and let it out slowly. "The last Saturday in March." He paused. "Of this year."

"This year?" the twins said in unison.

"Yes," Bliss supplied when Bobby seemed unable to speak. "Mr. Tratelli had a wedding planner, but the gentleman seems to have left town. He was only recently made aware of this. Isn't that right, Bobby?"

Isabelle's eyes narrowed. "You mean you got stiffed by your planner?" When Bobby nodded, she gave her sister a look. They spoke in rapid-fire French for a moment before Isabelle said, "We got to help him."

"I suppose we do." This from Isolde.

"It'll cost extra, of course," Isabelle said.

Bobby exchanged an I-guessed-as-much look with Bliss. "I understand."

Isolde set the scissors down and reached for a pen. "Where's the ceremony?"

"Our church is in Latagnier, the one on Bayou Nouvelle near the old Breaux place. They'd originally planned to have the reception in the garden there, too, but the so-called wedding planner took off with the down payment." Bobby clapped his hands at his sides. "Another bride reserved the date for her wedding."

"And what else has been done?" Isabelle asked.

"I'm not sure." Frowning, he looked to be trying to remember. "I know the dress is at Neecie's place in Latagnier."

"Neecie's Place?" Isolde shook her head, and her extension cords swayed. "I don't know no Neecie's Place."

"Wedding Belles," Bliss supplied. "That's the name of it."

"That's right." Bobby gave her a grateful look and said, "Thank you."

"We can find that one in the phone book, yes?" Isolde said.

"Yes," Bliss offered. "Or I can give it to you."

"Please, yes, do that, hon. Now, is there anything else you can tell us?" Isabelle said.

"Anything else?" Bobby looked toward Bliss with a helpless stare. "Do you know of anything else?"

"Like what?" Bliss asked.

"Colors, music preferences, all that stuff, eh?" Isolde said as Isabelle nodded in agreement. "We need something to work with, *cher*, lessen you want us to make it all up."

"We could do that," Isabelle said, "but you might have ideas of your own. Say, handsome, where is that daughter of yours? Maybe we ought to talk to her."

"She'll be back in a week. I'm taking care of this for her."

"Well, that explains why you don't got no wedding plans and it's less than a month before the wedding," Isolde said.

"Hush, sister," Isabelle scolded. "We don't talk to the customers that way, you hear?" She offered Bobby a smile. "Now, you got something to show us on what's been done?"

"Anything will do," Isolde echoed.

Bobby snapped his fingers. "I've got a folder out in the truck. Just a sec," he said as he went bounding outside.

"Oh my," Isabelle said. "He is a fine-lookin' man, Bliss. Are you certain you two are not a couple?"

"Yes, ma'am, I'm certain."

Isolde made her way around the counter, holding the cords

up high to keep from tripping. "Are you crazy in the head, girlie?" She tossed her orange necklaces around her neck, then grabbed Bliss's hands. "The Lord, He don't have any accidents, *non*?"

"*Non*. I mean yes." Bliss shook her head. "What I mean to say is, of course He doesn't make any mistakes."

"That's right," Isolde said. "Now I'm gonna done tell you if you don't listen the first time to my advice, you gone done missed it." She wagged a gnarled finger at Bliss. "The Lord, He done tole me that man out there's the one for you. Mark my words. You gonna need a wedding planned before long."

The bell rang, indicating that Bobby had returned. "Here's the file." He held up a blue folder. "Something blue," he said with a shrug.

When neither woman got the joke, Bliss stepped in. "Could we sit somewhere?"

"Oh, that's right," Isolde said. "You the cripple girl."

The words cut like a knife through Bliss's heart. Before she could speak, Isabelle came to her rescue.

"Pshaw, sister," she said. "She's fit as a fiddle. Can't you see that?" She turned her attention to Bobby. "You, big handsome man. You want some coffee?"

When Bobby declined, Isabelle pointed to a table and chairs in the corner. "Go plant yourself over there, and we'll get the books."

At first he didn't seem to understand. "Wait," he said slowly, "so you'll definitely take on the challenge? You're going to plan the wedding?"

"It won't be cheap," Isabelle said with a snort. "But from the look of your truck, I think you can afford it."

"That's right, what she said just now," Isolde repeated. "We'll do it, but it's gonna cost you."

❧

"She wasn't kidding when she said it would cost me."

Bobby sat across from Bliss at Richards on the Atchafalaya River. The food at the quaint local hangout was good enough to draw people more than four miles off the freeway, down a road so tiny that one car had to pull off the road to allow an oncoming vehicle to pass.

They'd been fortunate enough to snag a table overlooking the Atchafalaya River, but Bobby's focus was elsewhere—a pity, considering the beautiful scenery and the excellent quality of the shrimp toast appetizer.

"But, hey, I've got a wedding planner, and that's what counts," he added.

"You've got *two* wedding planners," Bliss reminded.

"Yeah, double the fun," Bobby said with a grin. "Thank you for coming with me. I was lost after the first five minutes." He paused. "Can you really tell the difference between ecru and off-white?"

"Oh, Bobby, is there really a difference between a chain saw and a table saw?"

"Point well taken." He reached for his water glass and held it high. "To weddings," he said.

"To weddings," she repeated as their glasses clinked. Then she took a sip.

Their attentive waiter swooped in to refill their glasses. "Ah, you two are celebrating?"

"We are," Bobby said. "I thought it was impossible, but it looks like there will be a wedding next month."

"Next month. Congratulations." He hurried off to the kitchen before Bobby could respond.

"Bobby, I think he thought *we* were planning a wedding."

"We are," he said, "or rather, I am." Shrugging, he reached for a piece of shrimp toast. "I know I've said it more than once, but thank you for coming with me."

"Enough. Despite what I've said to the contrary, I had nothing better to do today. Showing me this great little place for lunch is payment enough, all right?"

He ducked his head. "All right."

"Good. Now that we agree, how about we change the subject?"

"I can do that. It has occurred to me that you know all about what's happened with me since graduation." Bobby set his fork down and rested his elbows on the table, turning his attention fully to Bliss. "But I don't know more than a thing or two about you."

"There's not much to tell."

"Oh, come on," Bobby said. "I do know that you graduated with honors from LSU and ended up at the Bentley in Austin."

"Yes," she said cautiously, "that's true."

"And I know you opened the Cake Bake a little over two weeks ago."

"True again."

With those statements, Bobby exhausted the entire body of facts she felt comfortable discussing. With any luck, he'd missed the clue left by the sisters. The last thing she wanted to discuss was her health.

And yet, if he asked, she knew she would tell him. This was Bobby Tratelli, the chubby tagalong and persistent shadow who was now all grown up. She cut him a sideways glance. Yes indeed, he was all grown up.

"So, what happened in between?"

Thankfully, a gentleman with a large mustache and Elvis sideburns strolled up and settled into the chair between them. "I understand we have a wedding in the works," he said as he toyed with the ends of his extensive but well-groomed facial hair.

"Yes," Bobby said, "we have." He glanced over at Bliss. "Bliss, this is our host, James Berlin. James, may I present Bliss Denison? She and I are childhood friends."

"And I've known Bob since his cowboy days."

"He was an extra on the movie I told you about." Bobby elbowed James. "Now he fancies himself a restaurant owner."

"Among other things." James shook Bliss's hand. "So, tell me. What does a lovely lady like you see in a fellow like Cowboy Bob here?"

"What?" She looked at Bobby. "Do you know what he's talking about?"

Bobby chuckled. "James, I think you misunderstand. Amy's getting married, not me."

"Your baby girl? Impossible."

"Sad but true. My baby girl's vice president of Tratelli Aviation now, and much as I hate to admit it, in a few more years, she's probably going to end up being a better pilot than her old man."

"Is that possible?" James laughed. "What I don't understand is how our children grow older and we don't."

"Let me know if you figure it out," Bobby said.

Bliss's phone rang, and instinctively she reached for it. "Would you two excuse me? This is my mother."

"Of course," James said.

"Tell her I'll be back in the office soon."

"Okay," she said as she answered the phone.

"Bliss, are you all right?"

She cut a glance at the men, now engrossed in an animated conversation about a newborn colt. "I'm having lunch right now, Mama."

"Well, can you step away from the table for a minute? I've got something to tell you that won't wait." Bliss moved to a quieter corner of the lobby. "All right, Mama, this better be good."

"It's good, all right."

"Mama, please. Don't you have to work?" She stepped farther back out of the way to let a trio of chattering customers pass. "Oh, and I understand congratulations are in order. Bobby said you struck a hard bargain before you agreed to work for him."

"Pshaw, I would've done this job for nothing just to get out of the house, but I'd never admit that to him. Now let me tell you about Neecie before the phones start ringing again."

eleven

"Bliss, you've been quiet since you finished that call. Are you all right?"

What to say? The Latagnier city limit sign loomed large ahead. Another five minutes, ten at the most, and she'd be home. She risked a glance at Bobby. Unfortunately, he caught her looking.

"No," she said slowly, "I'm not all right. That call from Mama? She had quite a story to tell, and I'm still trying to figure it all out."

"Nothing wrong at the office, I hope."

"Actually, no."

"Home?"

"Can't say. Sorry."

Bobby shook his head. "Well, that's pretty vague."

"I know, but it's the best I can do right now. I'm really sorry. I wish I knew more." Bliss held her breath and waited for Bobby's next question. When he chose silence, she exhaled and leaned against the seat. A few minutes later, he pulled the truck to a stop in front of the Cake Bake.

"Hey, looks like Neecie's back," he said. "Maybe I ought to go pick up Amy's dress while she's open."

"Mama said she delivered it to the office."

"She did?" He smiled. "That was real nice of her."

"It was, wasn't it?"

"I know I've thanked you a dozen times," he said.

She held her hand up to silence him. "I enjoyed it," she said "Really. And thank you for lunch. Your friend is quite a character."

Bobby chuckled. "That's the truth. Well, I suppose I should get back to the office."

"I'm sure Mama's got everything under control."

"Oh, you know it," Bobby said.

Bliss stepped out of the truck and waved as Bobby pulled away. Once he rounded the corner, she tossed her keys into her purse and headed next door to Wedding Belles.

If Mama's scoop was right, she would find her answer somewhere in the store. As it turned out, she had to go no further than the cash register. There stood Neecie with a diamond the size of a small rock on her left hand.

"All right, girl," Bliss said, "what gives?" She pointed to Neecie's ring.

The color drained from Neecie's face, and she quickly slipped the ring into the front pocket of her jeans. "You didn't see that," she said. "Please just tell me you didn't."

"I did," Bliss said, "and so did Mama when you went out to Tratelli Aviation to deliver Amy's dress."

Neecie gripped the edge of the counter until her knuckles matched her face. In the background, the sound system played "In the Garden."

"It's not a new ring, you know. It's old. I just don't wear it. Much." Neecie's eyes shut, and she sank onto a stool. "I can't believe I was so stupid."

"What's going on, Neecie? First you disappear; then you come back with what's obviously a diamond ring on your left hand." She paused, sensing Neecie's extreme upset. "You know what? It's none of my business. It's just that Mama was worried. She's got some crazy theory about your ex that she refuses to elaborate on. Now personally, I don't see what's so wrong with this, but Mama, well, she seems to think it's a disaster."

Neecie pressed her lips into a thin line. She opened her eyes and stared at Bliss without expression.

"Suit yourself, Neecie. What do I know? I don't even have an ex. Personally, I figure if a man's worthy of it and God's in it, there's nothing wrong with returning to a love when the timing is a little more right."

She turned to leave the shop only to hear Neecie call her name. When she whirled around, her friend had begun to make her way toward Bliss.

"I'm in trouble, Bliss." She fell into Bliss's arms and began to cry. "I love him," Bliss thought she heard her say. "I'm so stupid."

"You love whom?" Bliss patted her back and tried to think. "Neecie, is this the father of your children we're talking about?" Bliss felt rather than saw her nod. "Then what's the problem?"

"You've obviously been out of town, Bliss. Everyone in Latagnier can tell you the problem."

"I'm not asking everyone in town. I'm asking you." Bliss looked around the shop, then linked arms with Neecie. "Come on home with me, and let's have some tea."

"But the shop. I've already been away too much."

"Do you still have that emergency sign?" When Neecie nodded, Bliss continued. "Then grab it and tape that thing on the door. What you need is a cup of tea and some girl talk."

Neecie almost smiled. "Do you have any more of those pralines? They were really good."

"Absolutely." She urged Neecie to follow her. "Now, come on. Let's get out of here before a wedding emergency breaks out."

A cup of tea and a half dozen pralines later, Neecie was ready to talk. "So, when I married him, I thought it was forever. I mean, you don't go into a marriage thinking you can just leave anytime you get ready to, right?"

"Right," Bliss said.

Her friend reached for another praline and nibbled on it. "See, that's what I thought, too, but people change. Situations change. Sometimes you have to let them go, right?"

"Neecie, what are you talking about?" Bliss reached for her napkin and dabbed at the tears streaming down Neecie's face. "You're not exactly making sense, honey."

"I'm not, am I?" She blew out a long breath, then smoothed back her hair. "Okay, we go way back, right?"

"Right."

"Then will you just do me one favor?"

Bliss's face clouded with worry. "Is it legal?"

Her friend almost smiled. "Of course. It's just that I have to get out of town for a few days." She held up her hands as if to stop a response from Bliss. "I know I've already been gone, but, well, this is something I have to do."

"How can I help?"

"This afternoon I delivered all the dresses with completed fittings. My mother will keep an eye on the kids, but I can't ask her to do that and watch the store." She gave Bliss a doubtful look. "Saturday's my biggest day of the week, and I know you're not open that day, so I was wondering if maybe you could. . ."

The strong urge to say yes was tempered by the fact she'd made several promises to the contrary. "Oh, honey, I'm sorry. I just can't."

"I understand." Neecie shook her head. "I shouldn't have asked. It's too much to—"

She promised her doctors and mother she'd stick to a part-time schedule, but Neecie didn't need to hear about Bliss's health problems at the moment. Bliss managed a smile. "No, it's not that. But," she quickly added, "I wouldn't mind answering your phone and taking messages. Do you think you'll be back by Monday?"

She nodded. "I promised Mama I'd be back for church on Sunday. It's the only way she would watch the kids. If things go the way I expect, I could be back well before then."

Bliss searched her friend's face. "Honey, are you sure you're doing the right thing?"

Neecie gave a wry chuckle. "Bliss, you don't even know what I'm doing."

"No, and I'm not asking you to tell me. What I'm asking is whether you've prayed about this."

"Constantly," she said as she rose to deposit her cup in the sink. "Actually, I'm looking forward to the day when I don't have to pray about this." Neecie paused. "I guess that'll never happen."

"The Lord does say we should pray without ceasing. I guess that pretty much means all the time."

Neecie smiled. "I guess so. Anyway, I've got a few loose ends to tie up over at the shop; then I'll be on my way." She headed for the door, then called over her shoulder, "I'll be sure Mama knows to drop the phone off here tomorrow when she leaves."

"That'll be fine," Bliss said. "And, Neecie?"

"Yes?" she said from the door.

"I don't know anything about what's going on with you, but it seems to me that there can't be a problem with a woman still loving the father of her children after all these years. I mean, how is that so bad?"

"You're right about one thing, Bliss." Neecie gripped the door frame. "You *don't* know what's going on." She paused. "And if you don't mind, I'd rather keep it that way. I like it that you still respect me."

For a long time after Neecie had gone, Bliss continued to stare at the door and the activity on the street beyond. Her friend was in trouble; that much seemed obvious. What sort of trouble was definitely something Neecie could and should keep to herself.

Bliss turned the lock on the door and hit the lights, then hauled her aching body upstairs and kicked off her shoes. The walk this morning had her legs complaining, but it was a small price to pay for finding out she had more stamina than she expected. At this rate, Bliss decided as she padded across her tiny living room, she'd be running a mile before her birthday.

She sank onto the sofa and reached for the remote, turning channels until she found a news program. Maybe on Saturday she'd go to the Shoe Shack and pick up a new pair of running shoes.

"No," she decided. "I think I'll go to that place in New Iberia that fits them to your feet." Bliss smiled. "Yes, that's what I'll do. I'll treat myself."

All day Friday, as she filled orders for cakes and pastries to be picked up for weekend events, Bliss thought about her trip to town. New running shoes were a graduation gift, of sorts. She hadn't bought a pair since the accident.

How long had she lived as if her life were over? In truth, much of what she knew to be normal was gone, but a few things remained: family, Latagnier, and the ability to run.

That last one would take a bit of effort and training, but with care and perseverance, she'd accomplish it. Of this, Bliss had no doubt.

Saturday morning, Bliss hurried through her oatmeal and toast, then set off for New Iberia. It was a glorious day, the first weekend in March, and she rode all the way with the sunroof open and the heater on. After she purchased a pair of runners in blue and white, she decided to break them in by doing some window shopping in town.

Depositing the bag containing her old shoes in her car, she set off down the sidewalk at a brisk pace. The shoes felt good, and so did the exertion. As always, she paid close attention to her heart rate and breathing.

She picked up her pace, shedding her jacket to tie it around her waist. By the time Bliss reached the city park, she knew a rest was in order, however, so she settled onto the park bench across from the old five and dime building to people watch.

Grandma Dottie used to bring her to this very park, this very bench, years ago. As a child she hadn't appreciated the time spent sitting on the bench. Rather, she preferred to race across the grass-covered divide, chasing imaginary friends and making real ones. Often, when Mama was busy at the sawmill, she and Grandma Dottie would make bologna and mayonnaise sandwiches and pack them in the hamper along with homemade dill pickles.

Her grandmother didn't much care for store-bought food, but the one exception was the bags of potato chips they'd purchase at Mulatte's Corner Market. Bliss had two jobs on these outings: purchasing the chips while Grandma Dottie waited outside and pressing the wrinkles out of the old tablecloth so Grandma Dottie could set out the meal.

The only item she'd requested from her grandmother's estate had been the old tablecloth they had used to spread on the grass for their feasts. It now rested in a place of honor on her cypress sideboard.

Maybe someday she would find a use for it again.

Bliss sighed. The odds were certainly not with her on that.

Lord, it's a silly request—nothing like finding world peace or saving souls—but would You consider sending me someone who likes an occasional picnic?

A check of her watch told Bliss it was time to head back to Latagnier. If Mama found out she'd gone to New Iberia without her, Bliss would never hear the end of it.

Better to slip back into town undetected than to have to explain why she ventured to the site of Mama's favorite shoe shop without her. Bliss smiled. What other middle-aged woman had to hide a trip to town from her mother?

Funny how normally she would've welcomed her mother's company. Today, however, she craved the quiet. On the return trip to Latagnier, she turned off the radio and enjoyed the silence.

It wasn't until she got back home that she realized she'd left without grabbing Neecie's phone. Sure enough, there were three missed calls.

Bliss kicked off her shoes under the front counter and reached for paper and pen. "What am I thinking? I don't have a clue how to retrieve her messages." She reached for the phone book to call Neecie's mother, only to find that Mrs. Trahan didn't know how to retrieve Neecie's voice mail messages, either.

The only thing she could do was record the numbers for Neecie, then return the calls. The first number belonged to a woman who needed to schedule a fitting, and the second was a wrong number. The third, it turned out, belonged to Bobby.

"I'm sorry," she said. "I didn't recognize your number, and neither Neecie's mother nor I could figure out how to pick up her voice mails."

"I just wanted her to know that the ladies from Divine Occasions were going to call her one day next week. Something about matching the flowers to the bridesmaid dresses, I think. Or maybe it was the tuxes." He laughed. "Anyway, I figured Neecie might want a heads-up on that since Isolde made it sound like this was a big deal."

Bliss joined him in his laughter. "How about I just leave Neecie a message that she's going to be getting a call from your new wedding coordinators next week about color details?"

"Sounds good. And, Bliss?"

She stopped scribbling. "Yes?"

"I really appreciate you going with me to Lafayette. Isabelle told me yesterday that they agreed to do the wedding because they remembered you and your mother." He paused. "Evidently you made quite an impression on them."

"Well, isn't that nice?"

"Yes, but there's just one thing that confused me."

Bliss set the pen down and leaned against the counter. "What's that?"

Bliss felt her shoulders slump.

"Why do they call you the crippled girl?"

Bliss felt her shoulders slump.

"Bliss?" Bob leaned against the fender of his truck and waited for her to respond. "Hey, are you there? Did we get disconnected?"

"I'm here."

Uh-oh. He hadn't been a husband for a long time, but it didn't take much man sense to know that he'd ventured into dangerous territory.

Staring at the back of the house, he tried to figure a way out of the quicksand he'd just stepped into. No way to do it but through it—that was his dad's motto. Best make his apologies, then change the subject.

He'd had Bliss on his mind anyway, as much for her opinion of Amy's latest stalling tactics as for the need he had to hear her voice again.

Bob cleared his throat and took a stab at saying he was sorry. "Look, that was a dumb question. Either they're remembering the wrong person or I'm out of line in asking. In either case, forget I said anything, okay? I actually could use your advice on something, so I'm really glad you called."

"What can I help you with?" she said in a small voice.

"It has to do with Amy." He turned around to rest his elbows on the hood of the truck and his gaze on the new foal prancing with his mama in the pen. "She called last night."

"Is something wrong?" The concern in Bliss's voice couldn't be missed.

"Well, she says there isn't, but she was supposed to be flying back tomorrow."

"And?"

The mare tossed her mane, then gave the colt her attention.

"And I'm wondering what you think about that."

"What did she say, exactly?"

"Just that she was delayed. That was her exact word: *delayed*." He shook his head and closed his eyes. "I've got a bad feeling about this, Bliss. I'm wondering if I ought to call the whole thing off."

"Why don't you just call and ask her?"

He opened his eyes, then blinked to adjust to the blinding sunlight. "Now why didn't I think of that?"

The answer to his question came in the form of a most feminine giggle. "Call her, Bobby," she repeated. "Tell her your concerns and be completely honest. And ask her point-blank if she wants you to call off the wedding."

After another few minutes of making small talk with Bliss, Bob did just that. "Hey, sweetheart," he said when he heard his little girl's voice on the line. "How's my princess today?"

"Your princess is tired," she said. "I had no idea how much walking I did today until I quit. Now I'm sitting in my hotel room too tired to draw a bath."

"Poor baby," he said. "Did you have a good day?"

"I had an amazing day."

"Tell me about it," he said as he walked toward the pen. "What did you and Chase find to do in Paris today?"

"Chase had to work."

"I see," he said as he tested the strength of the gate. "So what did you do all alone in London?"

For the next half hour, Amy told him all about her adventures. By the time she finished, he'd fed the chickens, made coffee, and put a steak on to grill.

He punched the button on the microwave to start the potato cooking, then stepped out of the kitchen to settle in his favorite chair on the deck. "So you did all that by yourself?"

"Daddy, please, I'm not twelve."

And yet something in her tone told him it might be.

twelve

"All right, sweetheart," Bob said. "Suit yourself. I guess I was just a little surprised that Chase wasn't with you, especially since the idea of staying over was to spend time with your fiancé."

"It was." She paused. "Look, we will have plenty of time to spend together on our honeymoon. I know he won't be working on an audit then."

"Are you sure?" Bob watched a pair of scissor-tailed flycatchers swoop and dive at the far end of the pasture. Likely as not, there was a new nest out there somewhere.

"Daddy, what are you saying?" Her voice went up an octave, putting him in mind of all the times she'd expressed indignation at some offense her father committed. Back then it had been such travesties as forgetting to wake her up in time to wash her hair before school or daring to tell her that the shorts she wanted to leave the house in were staying home without her. "Daddy?"

He shook his head and prayed for the right words to come. "Honey, I need to say something to you, and I want you to hear me out before you answer. Okay?"

"Okay," she said in a tentative tone.

"Okay. And when I finish, I want a truthful answer, even if it's not the answer you think I want. Deal?"

"Always," she said.

"All right." Bob took a deep breath, let it out slowly, and then forged on. "Amy, I like Chase just fine. He's a good man, hardworking, and an all-around nice guy. A father couldn't ask for a better provider for his daughter." He paused. "But, honey, are you sure he's the one? Are you 100 percent certain Chase Cooper is the man God wants you to marry?"

"Daddy, stop worrying about me."

"Amalie Clothilde Tratelli, answer the question."

Silence.

"Amy?"

"I'm here, Daddy." He could hear her sigh. "I'm tired. Can we talk about this tomorrow?"

"No, Amy. Right now. If Chase is not the man you're supposed to marry, then I'll make a couple of calls and the wedding will be off."

"Yes," she finally said. "I think Chase Cooper is the man God wants me to marry." Another pause. "Happy?"

"It's not about me being happy, sweetheart. This is about you being happy. That's all I ever wanted for you." He cleared his throat and tried to find his voice. "I promised your mama I would see to your happiness, and I'm not going to let her down. So, when're you coming home? If you leave me alone to handle this wedding much longer, there's no telling what will happen."

"Daddy, stop worrying. I believe in you; you'll make this day the most amazing of my life. Now, tell me about this new wedding planner you hired."

"Planners, actually. Their names are Isabelle and Isolde, and they're twin sisters. They run a place called Divine Occasions, and they've got everything under control. Bliss and I drove over to Lafayette to meet them, and they seemed to know what they were doing."

"That's a relief." She paused. "So, tell me about this Bliss person."

Bob chuckled. "This Bliss person is Bliss Denison. She and I went to high school together. She's recently come back to Latagnier. She owns the cake shop next to Wedding Belles."

"I think I met her the day before I left. She was having

coffee with Neecie when I went in for a fitting. She's a pretty lady."

"I suppose."

"And you've spoken a lot about her in the last couple of phone calls."

Bob shifted in his chair and set his sights on the horizon. "Have I?"

"Daddy, are you interested in her?"

"Interested?" he sputtered. "Bliss is an old friend, nothing more. I'm too old to be interested in anything but a good steak and a soft recliner."

"Methinks thou doth protest too much." She giggled. "You *are* interested in her. I can hear it in your voice."

"I called to talk about you, not me. Now, honey, I'm going to give you one more chance to pull the plug on this shindig. Do you want to marry Chase the last Saturday in March, or would it be more advisable to postpone the wedding for a while?"

"Thanks to my amazing father and the help of the ladies at Divine Occasions, I'm marrying Chase the last Saturday in March. All I have to do is drag him away from his audits."

"Amy."

"Daddy! I was kidding!"

But was she? The question dogged him the rest of the evening, rendering even the best chicken he'd grilled in ages tasteless. Finally, he paid one last visit to the mare and her colt before heading up to bed.

As he laid his head on the pillow, Bob closed his eyes—not to sleep, but to pray. He ticked down the list of concerns, starting as he always did with Amy, then his parents, and on down the line. Just before he said, "Amen," he slipped in a prayer for Bliss that sent him to sleep with a smile on his face.

The next morning, the smile remained. He'd dreamed about horses and London and, strangely, Bliss. Amy had been in the dream, too, but only as an observer. The odd thing was, at the end, it was he and Bliss who walked down the aisle at the church and not Amy and Chase.

All during Sunday service, the dream teased at the corners of his mind, fighting a sermon on tithing for his attention. Bliss wasn't in attendance this morning, but then he'd discovered she generally attended the later service.

He might have called her to grab a bite of lunch, but there were too many tasks on his to-do list and not enough hours to get them accomplished. Knowing that on Monday morning he would pay for his time spent on the wedding last week, Bob decided to pass the afternoon in a less taxing manner.

"There's just something about a Sunday afternoon nap that makes the whole week ahead look brighter," he muttered as he settled into the recliner.

When thoughts of Bliss crowded out any plans for a nap, Bob gave up and headed out to the airport to putter around in the hangar. One hour turned into four, and before he knew it, his stomach complained and he realized he'd missed dinner.

A grilled cheese sandwich and a bag of chips later, Bob climbed back into the recliner, the remote control in his hand. As his eyes closed during a commercial break of his favorite mystery show, he promised himself he would rest them for just a moment.

When the phone rang, he nearly jumped out of his skin. It took him a full minute to realize where he was and to whom he was speaking.

"Everything's fine, Mama," he said as the awareness of his surroundings gradually returned. "We had a near disaster when the wedding planner skipped town; I've hired another firm, though, and we're back in business."

"Oh, honey, I should be there," his mother said. "I can be on a plane home tomorrow."

"Don't you dare do that. Pop would have my hide if I

hauled you back here before the end of your visit." He paused to set down the remote he'd been holding. "Amy's not here anyway, so I don't know what you'd be doing."

"Amy's not there?" his mother said. "Where is she?"

"In London with Chase."

"Now isn't that interesting! In my day, the honeymoon came after the wedding."

"It's not a honeymoon, Mama. Amy was working in London, and Chase was sent to London to do an audit. When Amy completed her work, she stayed in London to spend time with Chase."

"Well, isn't that nice! I'm sure they're having a wonderful time together."

Bob shook his head. "No, actually it sounds like Amy has spent very little time with Chase, although she says she's having a blast."

"Now isn't that interesting!"

"Mama, you're repeating yourself." Bob sat forward in the recliner and pushed to his feet.

"I might be repeating myself, but I do find it interesting that the bride-to-be is spending so much time alone and doesn't seem to mind it a bit." His mother paused. "How involved has she been in the wedding of late?"

"Involved?" He stretched the kinks out of his back as he clicked off the television and set the remote on the table. "What do you mean?"

"I mean, has she been participating in the planning of this thing, or is she letting you handle it?"

Bob hesitated. "Well, at first this wedding was all she talked about. Remember?"

"Oh, I do." Mama chuckled. "She and I had some long talks about it way back when he gave her that ring. Amy had definite ideas about what she wanted that wedding to be like."

"Yes, well, I'm not so sure how much she cares about that

right now." He sighed. "Mama, I don't know what to do. I've got some concerns. I told her that when I talked to her. I offered to let her walk away from this marriage for now and told her I wouldn't be the least bit upset with her."

"What did she say?"

"She said that she feels like Chase is the man God wants her to marry." He paused. "How can you argue with that logic?"

"You can't, honey," Mama said. "So you've got to trust and let go. Oh, and to pray that the Lord will close this door if it's one our Amy isn't supposed to walk through."

"Well, I can't argue with that, either." He chuckled. "I guess I ought to count myself lucky that I am surrounded by smart women."

"Not lucky," his mother said, "but blessed. So, tell me about this woman you've been seeing."

"Woman?"

"Oh, don't play coy with me, son," Mama said. "Latagnier's a small town. I knew you were having coffee with Bliss Denison before it was cool enough to sip without scalding your tongue."

All he could do was laugh. Sadly, his mother spoke the truth.

Bob stepped into the kitchen and put the phone on speaker as he began to prepare the coffeepot for tomorrow. He winced as he noticed the time on the microwave clock.

A quarter past eleven.

"So," she continued, "are you interested in Bliss?"

"You're starting to sound like your granddaughter."

"Oh," Mama said, "the smart one?"

"Very funny. She's your only granddaughter. Look, I've got to get to bed. It's two hours earlier out in California, and some of us have to work for a living."

"Work for a living? Son, you don't fool me for a minute."

"What are you talking about? You know how many hours I spend at the office."

"Oh, I surely do. Hours and hours, sometimes forgetting what time it is because you're so engrossed in something you're working on out at one of the hangars. Am I right?"

"You are," he said grudgingly. "But it is hard work."

"You don't have to convince me, sweetheart. I've been there since the beginning, you know." Mama chuckled. "You and your daddy are too much alike for me not to realize that what you might tell other people is work is really just the thing you love and get paid for. And you're also not fooling me about Bliss Denison."

"I could remind you that we're just old friends," Bob said, "but that wouldn't do any good, would it?"

"My memory's just as sharp as it's always been, and I remember how you used to moon over that girl while she spent all her time trying to catch the attention of the Gallier boy," Mama said. "Did I hear that she's been helping you with the wedding plans?"

"She took a drive with me to Lafayette to speak to the wedding planner there. If I'd gone by myself, it would have been like sending a woman to buy power tools. Other than that, she's not any part of the wedding plans. Where did you get that information?"

"You know I can't reveal my sources. And shopping for power tools? That makes no sense, son," Mama said, "but nonetheless, I want you to remember she comes from a good family—and her mama and uncle were my best friends. Don't you dare be on anything but your best behavior around her."

"I'm not twelve." He cringed as soon as the words were out. Hadn't Amy just told him the same thing?

Fortunately, his mother responded with a giggle and a swift change of subject. After she'd recapped the Oscar ceremony and the various parties they'd attended, she hung up with the promise that she would be back in Latagnier in short order if she were summoned. She also stated she might come even if she weren't summoned.

Bob set the phone down and shook his head. How in the world did he end up in the middle of a group of strong-willed females?

Blessed? Maybe Mama thought so, but Bob had to wonder if his luck just hadn't run out.

That night he dreamed about London again, and this time he swooped Bliss off on a tour by horseback while the wedding planners followed, shouting questions about the color of carpet runners and the scent of candles. He woke up in a cold sweat and wondered once again about his luck.

"No, my blessings," he said as he rose to check how far from dawn the clock stood. "No sense going back to sleep now. I'd probably just have another crazy dream about the wedding." Bob yawned. "Once Amy gets back, this will all be her deal, and I can finally get some sleep."

Then it dawned on him. Amy never did say when she was coming home.

Bob grabbed for the phone and punched speed dial. He got Amy's voice mail.

"Probably out walking around London alone again," he muttered before hanging up. "Or maybe she got cold feet and is afraid to tell me."

The thought bothered him such that he paced the confines of his bedroom twice before calling her again. This time he let the voice mail pick up.

"Amy, this is your dad. I need to know when you're coming back, and I need to know today. You have to take over this wedding business. It's making me crazy."

Bob punched the button to end the call, then padded into the kitchen to make a pot of coffee. While he waited for it to perk, the phone rang. He raced back into the bedroom to pick it up just before it rolled over to the message.

"Amy?"

"Daddy, you have absolutely *got* to get control of yourself," she said. "I promise I will be home as soon as I can."

He ran his free hand through his hair and sighed. "Honey, I've got a bad feeling about all of this."

"Why?"

"I'm just afraid I'm going to mess something up. I'm no good at planning weddings."

Silence.

"The sooner you get home, the better it will be for all of us, understand? I don't plan weddings. I plan airplanes and I plan logistics for clients all over the world and I plan—"

"Okay, Daddy, I get it. You don't plan weddings, and I need to come home, like yesterday." She paused. "Look, I love you so much. I know you'll do a great job of handling this. You already have. Look at how you averted disaster by finding another planner."

Bob smiled despite himself. "I guess I did, didn't I?"

"See," she said. "So, I'm not worried, and you shouldn't be, either. I'm having an important dinner tonight with Chase and his boss. I know I need to be back in Latagnier, but I also need to be here for Chase. If I'm going to be his wife, I need to be willing to support his career, don't I?"

He was hard-pressed to find an argument for that question. Rather, he had to give her a grudging "Yes."

"Okay, so, after dinner Chase and I will make our plans to return. As soon as I know what those are, I'll call you and let you know."

"That's fine, honey, but I still have a bad feeling about this."

"Daddy! Now you're making me nervous. Stop, please."

"Sorry, sweetheart," he said quickly. "No matter what happens, your dad's in charge. It's going to be fine."

How could Bob promise Amy everything would be fine when

worry followed him like a cloud? He tried finding answers in his morning visit with God. Instead, the concerns grew.

The Lord was up to something. Either that, or some sort of disaster of epic proportions really was about to occur.

"Nothing I can do but wait and see what He's up to. Might as well do something to take my mind off it."

It was too early for watching the sports channel and too late to go back to bed even if he could. There was only one thing left to do.

Bob slid into his shorts and running shoes and threw on a sweatshirt, then headed out to pound some of his frustration into the dirt road that ran along the edge of his property. As he began his run, the sun teased the horizon and fought with the purple sky for a hold on the day. The air felt cool and dry, the wind blustery. He'd thought to take the old yellow Piper Cub out this morning, but the old girl would never stand up to the brisk March winds.

March.

The reminder of the fact it was his daughter's wedding month sent Bob rocketing forward, nearly doubling his pace from a slow jog to a full-on run. Chase was a good enough guy, not that any man would ever meet the standard he'd set for his one and only daughter.

But was he the right one?

"I don't guess anyone would be," Bob admitted through clenched jaw.

As he continued his bone-jarring pace on the rutted road, Bob thought back to his own wedding day and the squirming, crying mess Amy had been during the ceremony. "I'll be in that condition this time around," he said with a wry chuckle.

The road took a sharp turn to the left, but Bob ducked under the barbed wire fence and headed straight ahead across land belonging to his neighbors, the Breaux. The old schoolhouse lay just on the other side of the thicket, and on mornings like this, with patches of fog not yet burned off by the sun, he loved to challenge himself by running all the way out there and back by way of Bayou Nouvelle.

Bob picked his way across the old pasture, slowing his pace to allow for ducking around low-hanging limbs and the occasional sharp fronds of brilliant green palmettos. Finally, the old schoolhouse came into sight. The cedar siding and shake shingles were still wet with last night's heavy dew and this morning's accompanying fog.

He made two rounds about the house, scaring an old orange barn cat as Bob stomped past the woodpile, then veered off toward the bayou. Orange sparks flashed across the black water as the sun found its path above the tree line, and only the frogs complained. A golden-tailed squirrel skittered out of his path, sending a flock of marsh birds airborne.

Here the trail leveled out and the ruts were gone. The soft grass-covered path gave Bob just the right spring in his step, so he pushed forward to run once again at full speed.

Although his lungs burned with the exertion and the wind whipped across the bayou to sting his face, Bob felt great. Better than great.

When Bob reached this point, he knew he could run forever. He could take on the best of the best in any marathon. "Hey, maybe I will." Another few yards and he really began to like the idea. "Yeah, I can do this. I can run a—"

Then he tripped.

thirteen

The ground rose up to slug him square between the eyes, or at least that's the way Bob felt when he rolled up into a sitting position somewhere just south of the path he thought he knew so well.

He didn't realize he wasn't alone until a familiar female stalked into view. "Bliss? What are you doing here?"

"I was praying, Bobby," she said quite snippily. "And I was enjoying my quiet time until someone stomped on me."

"Stomped on you? Not hardly, Bliss."

"Then how do you account for the fact that I've got muddy shoe prints on my sweatpants."

He gave her a sideways glance, taking in her appearance, from the sweatpants and T-shirt and a sweatshirt tied around her waist to the ponytail that danced in the March wind. Indeed, Bliss looked dressed for running, but if that were the case, how could he have stumbled over her—literally? Still, that was the only explanation.

"Easy." He rubbed the spot where it hurt the most and felt a lump beginning to rise. "I was running along the path like any normal person when you tripped me."

"Tripped you?" She shook her head, and her mouth went wide. "I was sitting there minding my own business. Why didn't you announce yourself, Bobby?"

"Because I didn't expect anyone would have their legs stretched across the path, hidden behind a bush."

She knelt to massage her calf, and his heart sank. "Bliss, I'm an idiot. Are you all right?" He scooted over beside her. "I'm sorry. I've hurt you, haven't I?"

"Nothing like what I did to you." She touched his forehead, and a pain shot behind his eyes. "Oh, Bobby, you're bleeding. Here, let me see if I can help." Bliss shifted to her knees, untied the pink sweatshirt from her waist, and leaned over to dab at his forehead.

"It's nothing, I'm sure."

"It's blood, Bobby," she said as she continued ministering to the ache between his eyes. "And the presence of blood generally means it's *something*. Just relax and let me work."

But he couldn't relax. Not with Bliss so close. It was strange, the way her nearness made him feel. After all, this was Bliss. Sure, he had a thing for her for years, going way back to when they were kids. And sure, their friendship seemed on its way back to being what it had been when they were younger.

However, she'd never given him the time of day. No, Bliss Denison had been crazy about Landon, not him. Might still be for all he knew.

Which made the sudden desire to kiss her all the more odd. And appealing.

"Bliss." Bob encircled her wrist and pulled her hand away. Their gazes met. He folded the sweatshirt and handed it back to her. "Thank you," he managed, "but I'm fine now."

She looked as if she were going to say something. Then, slowly she nodded. "Yes, well, all right." She rose, but he sat where he was a moment longer. "I need to get back and clean up before it's time to open the store."

Bob nodded. "I think I'll just sit here awhile."

"Are you sure. . . ? Of course, you're fine."

He watched her take a few steps, then realized she was favoring one leg. "Bliss?"

His old friend turned. "Yes?"

"Quit pretending," he said as he struggled to his feet despite the jackhammers going off in his head.

"I could say the same for you." Her glare dissolved into a

giggle. "You're not hiding that headache very well."

Bob gestured toward her left leg. "You're not exactly disguising that limp, either." He nodded toward the south. "My house's a mile or so in that direction, maybe a little less. How about I drive you home?"

She pointed north. "My car's that way about a half a mile. You help me get there, and I'll drive *you* home."

He grinned and reached out to offer a handshake.

Bliss met him halfway and slipped her hand into his. "Deal," she said.

Rather than let her know he could have walked all day holding her hand, Bob released his grip. "Ready when you are," he said casually.

❧

Bliss felt like a first-class idiot. Who in the world falls asleep while praying outdoors? At home in her chair, okay, but here? And wouldn't you know it would be Bobby who tripped and fell over her?

So much for getting up early to try out her new shoes. From now on she would walk *after* work and not before.

Picking up her pace despite the throbbing in her calf, Bliss pushed away her humiliation to concentrate on the path ahead. Bobby easily kept up with her, occasionally stepping ahead to clear a limb or move an obstacle.

Not an easy task considering the goose egg on his forehead.

"So, Bliss," he finally said, "do you sleep outside beside the bayou often?"

Her cheeks flamed. "How did you know I was—"

"I didn't." His smile edged up a notch. "Thanks for confirming it."

"Hey." Bliss gave him a playful nudge, and then they walked along the bayou in companionable silence until the path turned and headed up an embankment.

Bobby jogged a few steps ahead, then reached down to

grasp Bliss's hand. "Here, let me help you."

Bliss looked up at Bobby, calculating the odds she would be able to make the climb without his assistance. It didn't take but a second to realize the truth and grasp onto her old friend's hand.

Her bad knee complained—and there would certainly be a nasty bruise on her calf—but she hid her pain and planted one foot in front of the other until she was once again on level ground. "Thanks, Bobby," she said. "I'm glad you were here."

He gave her a look. "Yeah, sure you are."

"No, really," she said as she fell into step beside him. "I don't think I could have climbed that without your help."

"And you wouldn't have had that problem if I had been watching where I was going." Bobby cringed. "I can't help but notice you're limping. I wonder if you might consider getting that looked at." He let out a long breath. "I just feel like an idiot for stomping on you like that."

Bliss stopped short and grasped her friend's hand. "Okay, enough of that. You aren't the reason I'm limping, okay?"

Bobby shook his head. "But you're going to have a bruise the size of my foot by bedtime."

The urge to change the subject or, worse, to agree with her old friend bore down hard on her. "Come with me," she said before she lost her courage. "I've got something to show you."

He looked skeptical but nonetheless followed her to the overturned tree trunk where she settled, then patted the place beside her. Without a word, she extended her leg and rolled up her sweatpants to reveal the ugly jagged scar, now nearly faded to white.

"I was in an accident. It changed my life."

She looked up to gauge Bobby's reaction, only to find him studying her face and not her scar. "I'm so sorry, Bliss." He reached for her hand and laced his fingers with hers. "Do you want to tell me about it?"

To her surprise, she did. "I worked late that night. I generally did in those days. Austin had a blue norther come through, so what passed for comfortable that morning was frozen over by that night. I was tired, and the light was yellow. I sped through it. They tell me the ice was the first thing I hit. All I remember was the railing on the Congress Street bridge coming at me." With those words came a torrent of others until the story of the accident was told.

All except for the part where the CAT scan showed she had a far more serious problem than the effects of an automobile accident. That nugget of information was best kept to herself, she decided. People tended to act differently when they found out she had the equivalent of a ticking time bomb in her body.

"So, that's how you ended up back here in Latagnier." He paused. "And that's why the ladies at Divine Occasions kept referring to you as. . ."

"As the crippled woman," she supplied. "Yes, when I first visited them, I was still dependent on my cane and brace. Thanks to physical therapy, I've come a long way since then."

"I can tell."

She paused. "Believe it or not, I drove into New Iberia and bought these new shoes on Saturday to celebrate the fact that I can actually walk a whole mile now without paying for it later. But today's actually the first day I got up early to do it."

Her friend fell silent, and Bliss felt like a fool for pouring out the gory details of her accident and its aftermath to him. She couldn't abide pity. Better to have remained silent, she decided, although the damage was obviously done.

"Would it be stupid of me to ask what you're thinking right now?" she finally said.

Bobby stared down at their entwined fingers, then lifted her hand to touch his lips. "What I'm thinking right now is that I wish I could take all of this pain away from you."

"Yes, well, God could have, but He didn't."

Bliss froze. She'd never said that aloud, never really admitted even to herself that she felt anger toward the Lord.

"I wish I had the answers," Bobby said gently, "but I don't. There are so many things I don't understand."

"Me, too," she said. "It's so hard not to get stuck asking why."

Bobby nodded and held her hand against his chest. "Sometimes asking why is what God wants, Bliss." When she gave him a confused look, he continued. "Not why it happened, but why God allowed it to happen. Asking Him why He saved us and not someone else. . ." He shrugged. "That's when it's okay to ask why. At least I think so."

Bliss looked down at the scar. Did God save her for a reason? He must have. She lifted her gaze to the heavens. *Someday, Lord, I'd just like to know why.*

"Sometimes, Bliss, God saves us not from the bad things in this world, but from ourselves." Bobby released her hand and cupped her chin, turning her face in his direction. "Could that be the reason? Did God need to save you from yourself?"

She peered at Bobby through a shimmer of tears. The depth of truth in that question stung as much as it soothed. "Yes," she whispered, "I think maybe He did."

Bobby wrapped her in an embrace and let her stain his shirt with her tears until she had no more to cry. Then, she lifted her head and stared up into the most incredible eyes.

"Thank you for listening," she said. "It's not a story I'm usually comfortable telling."

"Thank you," he said as he moved closer, "for trusting me enough"—he moved closer still—"to tell me."

And then, with exquisite slowness, Bobby fitted his lips over hers and kissed her.

"What just happened?" she whispered a moment later.

"Bliss, don't you recognize a kiss when you get one?" She pretended to consider the question while Bobby's smile lit up his face. "I guess I'll just have to try that again."

"I guess you will," she said. "That is, if you want to."

He closed his eyes as he said, "Oh yes, I want to." Then, to her surprise, he paused. "Bliss, open your eyes," he commanded.

She did.

"I want you to know you're kissing me." He smiled. "Kissing Bobby Tratelli."

Her heart thumped, and her mind raced. "No," she said.

Too soon, it was over. Bliss took a deep breath and let it out slowly while she sorted through her emotions.

"Bliss?" Bobby rose and reached for her hand, pulling her to her feet. "We both have places to be in, oh. . ." He checked his watch. "Half an hour."

"Oh no, is it that late?" She shook her pants leg back into position.

"Can I ask you something before we go? What just happened here?"

"You kissed me," Bliss said.

Bobby rolled his eyes. "I know that, but should I apologize?"

"I don't know. Can I get back to you on that?"

"You know it," Bobby said. "And in the meantime, I'm going to celebrate the small victories."

"What do you mean?"

Bobby enveloped her in an embrace. "My friend is back."

"Yes, that's true," she said.

"And I've been wanting to kiss you since third grade." He paused. "I guess that's a big victory."

"And the fact I'm back in Latagnier?"

He held up his thumb and forefinger and indicated a miniscule space between them.

"Stop teasing me," she said as she shared a laugh that faded to a smile as they walked back to her car.

That smile lasted throughout the morning despite the fact that she was late opening the shop and had to turn down three orders for wedding cakes on referrals. "I've got an opening in June," she said, "but only one date, so let me know."

Bliss hung up the phone and jogged back to the kitchen to silence the buzzer on the top oven. She'd already retrieved the cake and set it on the cooling rack when she realized she'd actually run.

It wasn't much, a trip measured in feet rather than miles, but it was the first time she'd run anywhere since the accident. She cast aside her oven mitts and tested her knee by flexing it. With only the slightest twinge of complaint, she accomplished the feat, then did it again.

"Thank You, Lord," she whispered as she went back to work. "Like Bobby said, sometimes we have to celebrate the small victories."

She flipped on the television and began the process of mixing the frosting for a groom's cake in the shape of a twelve-point deer. It was an interesting undertaking, transforming cake batter and cream cheese frosting into a creation fit for a man who planned every event around hunting season.

The morning talk shows dissolved into the noon news by the time Bliss completed the project. "And that's what you get when you marry a man who had a hunting license before he could ride a bicycle."

Bliss boxed up the cake and set it aside, tagging it with the order form and bill before moving on to the next item on the list: a two-tiered wedding cake covered in sugar hearts and topped with a mascarpone copy of the Volkswagen that caused the couple to meet.

She stacked the layers, anchoring them with frosting, then set about spreading the buttercream frosting. Just as a breaking news item about a shopping center fire came on the television, her phone rang. Bliss clicked the mute button and reached for her order pad. This time the caller was looking for a trio of cakes for a party taking place the first weekend in April.

"No, I'm sorry," she said, "there's no more availability. I've got one slot the week before Palm Sunday, but only for a standard cake. I can't do anything more complicated than that. For three cakes, I would have to block out an entire day. Would you like me to see when I can do that?" After hearing a yes from the caller, Bliss paused to check. "May 15 is the soonest."

The woman hung up with a promise to call back when she had a new date for the party. Bliss hit the mute button as the jingle from a grocery store commercial came on. A second jingle, one from the front door, pulled Bliss from the kitchen in time for her to see Neecie coming through the door.

"Hey, welcome back," she said.

Neecie looked tired, and Bliss bit her tongue to keep from telling her so. "Come on back here and have some coffee. I think I've still got some pralines, too. Or would you rather have tea?"

Her friend didn't say a word. Instead, she mutely followed Bliss into the kitchen, then dropped into the nearest chair. Bliss poured two cups of hot tea and set them on the table. Before Bliss knew what was happening, Neecie began to cry.

"Everyone in town thinks. . . Oh, Bliss, it's such a mess. I just want to keep things going the way they are because that's the easy way—I'll admit that—but I don't think the Lord will let me do it."

Bliss kept silent despite the questions swirling about in her mind. Instead, she reached for her napkin and dabbed at the tears streaming down Neecie's face. "You're not exactly making sense, honey."

"So when he called me to tell me, I said nothing," Neecie continued, "and did nothing. And now he's back, and I'm in a fix." She lifted tear-filled eyes to meet Bliss's gaze. "I don't know what to tell him. Worse, what do I tell the kids? Did you know I pulled out everything I had in savings and bought him a one-way ticket out of here? Anything to rid myself of a problem I honestly don't know if I mind having."

"Honey," Bliss said slowly, "didn't you hear me? I don't have a clue what you're talking about."

"She's talking about me."

Bliss nearly fell out of her chair when she looked up in the direction of the masculine voice and saw a stranger standing in the doorway. Obviously she'd been so focused on Neecie that she hadn't heard the bell ring or noticed the chirp of the alarm when the door opened.

Dark hair was cut close to his scalp and salted with gray, and his square jaw was clean shaven. The leather jacket and faded jeans gave him the look of a bad boy, but something in his expression conveyed the opposite.

"Did you tell her about me, Neecie?"

"Yes," Neecie said before dissolving into tears. "She knows."

"Wait." Bliss rose and set her napkin on the table beside her teacup. "What do I know? Say, you look awfully familiar. Do I know you?"

"I ought to look familiar, Bliss."

Something about the way the man said her name rang familiar. "How do I know you?"

"Remember the flaming flying bicycle?"

No. He couldn't be. "Landon?"

The man nodded.

"Landon Gallier? You're dead."

"No," he said. "I was stupid. I assure you I'm quite alive."

Bliss looked him over once, then turned to stare at Neecie. "You were married to Landon Gallier? How did I not know that?"

Landon shrugged. "It wasn't like we had a big church wedding or anything. Just a few folks in the pastor's study was what passed for a wedding for us, but we didn't care. Isn't that right, honey?"

Neecie seemed frozen in place. Finally, she nodded.

Bliss frowned. "Still, I can't believe I was so preoccupied with my career that I completely lost touch with people back home."

"You were busy," Neecie offered, "and you did so well for yourself at that hotel. Your mama was forever bragging about you."

"She was?" Bliss shook her head. "I want you to know that I'm never going to lose touch with where I came from, Neecie. I just won't let that happen again." She paused to look from Landon to Neecie. "So," she said slowly, "you were married to Landon."

fourteen

"*Is* married to me," Landon corrected as he crossed the room to rest his arm possessively on Neecie's shoulder. "We are *still* married."

Bliss struggled a moment to sort out her racing thoughts. She'd mourned a man who was now alive. On top of that, quiet and mousy Neecie had captured the quarterback. Both facts seemed just a little beyond believable.

"I'm sorry, Landon," Bliss said, "but I want to know the how and why of this. You have four children." She looked at Neecie. "The kids are his, right?" When Neecie nodded, she returned her attention to Landon. "Just exactly when did you figure out you weren't dead, Landon Gallier, and why is this woman upset by it?"

He looked down at Neecie. "What do I tell her?"

"Everything" came out as a rough whisper.

Landon sighed. "I was an idiot. A stupid drunk. I had a wife and kids, and all I wanted to love on was a bottle of bourbon. When I had a chance to travel, I took it. Then came the biggest opportunity of all. I got knocked off the rig and right into a new life."

Neecie began to wail, and Landon knelt to embrace her. "I'm so sorry, sweetheart. I'll use that plane ticket if you want, and no one has to know."

Bliss gave Landon a pointed look. "Neecie, do you want him to go?" When she said yes, Bliss rested her hands on her hips and gave him her most intimidating look—the one she used to reserve for kitchen help on their way to the unemployment office. "All right. Landon, I wonder if you might consider coming back another time. Obviously Neecie's not ready to talk to you right now."

Landon's handsome features contorted into what might have passed for anger, and Bliss felt the oddest slice of fear race through her heart. A moment later, he was smiling, no trace of the other emotion visible.

"What in the. . ."

Bliss turned around to see Bobby standing inches away from the door, his face white and his fists clenched.

"I was on my way to the post office and thought I might come by and take you to lunch," Bobby said. "I circled the block in time to see someone who looked an awful lot like my dead best friend, Landon Gallier, going into your shop, and I figured I'd check it out for myself. How've you been, Landon?"

"Oh, you know," Landon said as he hung his head. "I do okay."

"You always did, although coming back from the dead's a bit extreme, even for you."

"I deserve that." Landon shook his head. "In a sense, the man I was did die—in more ways than one."

"I'm listening," Bobby said.

"I wasn't the man I should have been. I was a lousy husband and a lousy father. When I woke up in that hospital with no name and no past, I decided I'd been given a second chance." He swallowed hard. "I figured Neecie and the kids were better off without me. I believed that until I met the Lord. That was four months ago. I've been trying to get the courage to come back ever since."

"Why did you come back?" Bob asked. "Why hurt everyone like this?"

He looked at Neecie. "I don't want to cause anyone any more pain. Neecie knows I've offered to disappear. I certainly don't deserve my family after what I've done."

"It's not about what any of us deserve," Bliss said.

"She's right," Bobby said. "Because if you got what you deserved, I'd already have slugged you, Landon. I'm glad you're alive, but I'm not so sure when I'm going to understand it."

"I want to do the right thing by Neecie and the kids. With Mom and Dad gone, there's no one else in this town who matters to me, other than maybe you two."

Neecie's weeping intensified, and Bliss ached to comfort her. Instead, she remained where she was and watched Landon embrace his wife.

"Landon?" Bliss finally said. "Do you have a place to stay?"

Landon nodded.

"Then you need to go there. Neecie obviously can't handle any more tonight. For that matter, neither can I."

"But, I—"

"Landon, go." Bobby's stance changed, accentuating the difference in size and temperament between the two men. "Bliss has already asked you, and now I'm *telling* you. Let's go."

Clearly the balance of power in the Landon–Bobby friendship had changed. Bliss watched in amazement as the former leader of their trio surrendered.

Landon paused, then nodded slowly. "I don't mean you any harm, Bliss," he said. "I just want my wife and kids back." His hand moved to caress Neecie's hair. "Neecie, we can be a family again. I'll do anything you ask to make that happen. I'm a different man now. A new man. The Lord saw to that. I can take that airline ticket you bought me and use it for a second honeymoon for us if you'll have me."

Neecie dipped her head and began to wail.

❧

"Let's go, Landon."

This time it was a demand and not a question. Bob had enough experience with women to know that when the waterworks started, a sensible man did all he could to stop the flow;

then, failing that, he bailed and let the womenfolk handle it.

Besides, if he stood here another minute, he wouldn't be responsible for his actions. Any man who would walk out on a life that included a loving wife and great kids didn't deserve anything but a solid slug between the eyes and a swift ride out of town.

He watched his formerly deceased buddy kiss the top of his wife's head, then give Bliss a quick hug. "I'm sorry to see you under these circumstances. I'd have preferred to get reacquainted under better conditions."

"Maybe another time, Landon." Bliss patted Landon's shoulder, then slipped out of his embrace. For a moment, Bob's old feelings of jealousy surfaced.

"Yeah," was Landon's gruff reply.

"How'd you get here?" Bob asked.

"Bus." Landon looked past Bliss to Neecie. "Even when I hated myself enough to disappear, I never stopped loving you, Neecie Gallier. Not one day went by that I didn't love you, but I knew it was better for all of you to have a happy memory of me rather than for anyone to know the truth about me."

Neecie didn't move. Didn't say a word.

"Landon," Bliss said softly, "please go."

"All right." Bob pointed to the door. "Time to go. You and Neecie can talk about this when she's ready. You hear?"

With only the slightest nod to let Bob know he agreed, Landon stuffed his fists in his pockets and headed for the door. Only after Bob had his buddy outside in the truck did he realize Landon was crying.

"Not you, too," Bob said as he reached into the console and grabbed a handful of fast-food napkins.

"Sorry. I was just thinking about how my wife bought me a plane ticket and told me to disappear. That's what she said when I called her and told her the truth about where I'd been the last ten months. She told me the kids didn't need me anymore and neither did she." Landon swiped his face, then wadded the napkins and tossed them on the floor of the truck.

"Hey, pick that up." He pointed to the mess at Landon's feet. "What do you think this is, your mama's house?"

Landon snorted a laugh. "If I'd tried that at my mama's house, she would've shot me."

"Funny, I was just thinking the same thing. And I'm a much better shot than your mother was." They drove in silence for a minute. "Where are you staying nowadays?"

Landon leaned back and stared out the window. "New Iberia."

"Then that's where I'll take you." He watched out of the corner of his eye to see Landon's reaction. All he saw was defeat. "Or is there somewhere else?"

"If I said my house, it wouldn't matter, would it?"

"I can't take you out there, and you know it." He paused. "Unless the kids already know you're back, too."

"No, they don't have a clue. I've respected Neecie's request to stay away from them." He continued to stare at the passing scene. "I guess maybe that's best. What do you think?"

"Best for a kid not to know his daddy's alive?" Bob drummed his fingers on the steering wheel, then signaled to turn at Evangeline Street. "No, I can't say as I believe that." He made the turn, then gave Landon a direct look. "You can have a future with your wife and kids, but you've got to do it the right way."

Landon shook his head. "What would you know? You've never done anything wrong in your life."

"That's not true. I've done things I'm not proud of."

Landon pointed to Bob's forehead. "Like whatever altercation landed that between your eyes?"

Bob touched the goose egg he earned that morning. "No," he said with a grin. "This one I *am* proud of."

Giving Bob a look of disbelief, Landon pointed toward downtown. "If you'd take me to the bus station, I'd sure appreciate it."

"No."

Landon gave him a startled look, then reached for the door handle. "I suppose I deserve that."

"Wait." Bob shook his head. "I won't take you to the bus depot, but I will take you back to New Iberia. You do still have a place to stay there, don't you?"

"Yeah," he said. "Until the end of the month, anyway." His old friend fell silent. "I wonder," he finally said, "if I could ask you something. A favor before we leave Latagnier."

"What's that?"

He swung his gaze to stare at Bob. "Would you drive me by my house?" He shook his head. "I mean, Neecie's house."

Bob thought about the request for a moment. "I don't know, Landon. What if someone sees you?"

He pointed to his watch. "School's in. No one should be home."

Grudgingly, he made a U-turn, then headed out toward the Gallier place. It didn't take long for him to reach the road leading to the home he'd done sleepovers in as a child more times than he could count.

"The old place looks good. Neecie must've hired someone to do the yard."

Bob grunted but said nothing. Landon wasn't really talking to him anyway. Sometimes a man needed to do things alone, even if he was in a car with other people.

Pulling the truck to the curb in a spot several houses down, Bob threw the gearshift into park. "You've got one minute," he said.

He glanced over at the house. Neecie had kept it up fairly well since Landon left. Other than the fact the shutters looked as if they could use a coat of paint, the place didn't appear much different than before he left.

Landon reached for the door handle, and Bob hit the lock. "Oh no you don't, pal. I said I'd drive you by. I didn't say I'd let you out."

"Fair enough." He leaned back again and closed his eyes. It was hard to miss the fact that he swiped at his eyes with the back of his sleeve. "Funny how life turns out, isn't it?"

"What do you mean?" Bob turned the truck around and aimed for the highway.

"I mean, things sure didn't end up like we all planned, did they?"

"No," Bob said slowly.

"I had plans of playing in the NFL. I was going to take Neecie on the ride of her life. The best hotels, the best cars, the best clothes." His laugh sounded hollow in the enclosed space. "It sure didn't turn out like that, did it?"

"It could have." Bob gripped the wheel. "It's all about what you choose to do with what you have. And it's about who you choose to follow."

He looked less doubtful than Bob expected. "I know." Landon paused. "All those years we were friends, all that time growing up here in Latagnier, well, I envied you, Bob. I can tell you that now."

He hadn't expected that.

"Me? Now that's a laugh. I was the fat sidekick. The shadow. You threw the touchdowns, and I took the hits." Bob took a deep breath and let it out slowly. "And no matter what, you were the one who always got the girl."

"And there were a whole lot of girls, weren't there?" He toyed with the door handle. "I always suspected Bliss might have had a thing for me." Landon shrugged. "I could've done something about it—almost did once, not all that many years ago."

"Is that so?"

"Yeah," came out like a long sigh. "It wasn't to be. Besides,

I always knew you were in love with her. I'm a creep, but I'm not that big of a creep." Another chuckle. "That's not exactly true. I *was* that big of a creep—once. Neecie thinks I still am. I never knew if she heard about the time I called Bliss in Austin thinking I was going to make up for lost time. I probably shouldn't tell Neecie now."

No response was necessary. Bob did, however, press a little harder on the gas pedal. The sooner he got Landon to New Iberia, the better—for both of them.

They rode for several miles in silence. Bob tried to pray, but the anger seethed too close to the surface. *I'm working on this, Lord*, was the best he could come up with. *Just let me get through this without punching the guy.*

Not soon enough, they arrived in New Iberia. Following Landon's directions, Bob ended up parked in front of a ramshackle A-frame with a sign out front declaring it the HARRISON HOUSE.

"Home, sweet home." Landon's hand reached for the door handle; then he froze. "You're going to think I'm really stupid."

"I already do, Landon."

His former friend ducked his head. "Yeah, well, here's the thing. I had my getaway completed. I was living the high life all boozed up and miserably happy. There was just one problem."

Bob's urge to slug Landon caused him to grip the arm of his seat. "Neecie and the kids?"

"No," he said. "Actually, it was something your dad used to say. Remember when he'd let us tag along out at the airfield? He always said, 'Boys, if you don't learn anything else in life, you need to learn that who you are is who you are no matter who's looking.'"

Despite himself, Bob chuckled at Landon's ability to mimic Pop. "Yes, he still tells me that."

"Well," Landon said slowly, "he's right. You really are who you are. Running from that doesn't change anything, except maybe to make things harder for the people who love you."

"Yeah, you definitely did that." Bob clenched his fists.

"I'm going to fix what I can and let the Lord do the rest." Landon paused. "And if I have to leave, I have to leave. I just want those I care about to know how sorry I am."

"Yeah, you're sorry all right."

"I deserved that," Landon said.

"That and more."

A long moment of silence fell between them. Bob knew better than to voice his thoughts, and Landon obviously felt the same. Eventually, Landon reached over to clamp his hand onto Bob's shoulder.

"Thanks for the ride." He shook Bob's hand, then climbed out of the truck. "Hey, I'm sorry you got messed up in my crazy domestic scene."

"You, Bliss, and me, we used to be a team. I'd do anything for the two of you."

Landon studied him a minute. "You would, wouldn't you?" He smiled. "You were always the better man, Bobby. Eventually, everyone who knew us figured that out."

After Landon closed the door and loped toward the entrance of Harrison House, Bob let out a long breath. "Yeah, everyone but Bliss."

Bob's phone rang, and he reached for it.

"Hi, Dad!"

He smiled. "Hey, sweetheart," he said.

"Daddy, we have a situation."

Her voice sounded so serious he almost laughed. Surely she was teasing him. "What's the situation?"

"You know Chase and I had dinner with his boss, right?"

"Right," Bob said.

"Well, Chase invited them to the wedding."

"That's wonderful, honey," Bob said. "What's the situation?"

"The situation is that now everything absolutely has to be perfect." She paused. "This is his boss, and his whole career is on the line."

"Over a wedding? Honey, I doubt—"

"I don't understand it, either," she said, "but Chase says it's of the utmost importance that this wedding comes off perfectly."

"All right," he said. "Calm down. I promise everything will be perfect, okay?"

"Okay. Have you talked to the wedding planners this week?"

"It's only Monday," he said with a chuckle. "We just spoke on Friday, but if it will make you feel better, I'll call them right now."

"It would, Daddy," she said. "You're the best," she added. "The very best."

Bob hung up feeling ten feet tall and bulletproof. As he scrolled through his address book looking for Divine Occasions, the office number appeared on his caller ID.

"What's up, Mrs. Denison?" he said when her voice came on the line.

"Are you listening to the radio, boss?"

"No."

"Well, tune in to the news station. There's a problem you need to know about."

❧

It took the better part of an hour, but Neecie finally calmed down enough to talk. "I don't even know where to start," she said as she sipped her tea. "Honestly, I thought you knew about Landon and me. I just figured you were being polite by not asking about him."

"Me, polite?" Bliss grinned. "Perish the thought. I just didn't think to ask, because believe me, I would have eventually."

Neecie smiled through the last of her tears. "I guess you must have a lot of questions."

"Well, of course I do, but what's the point in asking them until you're ready to give me lots of answers?"

Neecie rested her elbows on the old wooden table, then cradled her chin and sighed. "If I had one more praline, I might be able to find some of those answers."

Bliss smiled as she rose to reach for the container. Filling the platter, she set it in front of Neecie. "That enough?"

"Probably not," Neecie said, "but it's a start."

"So, I'll begin with the obvious. When did you and Landon become an item? When I left for college, you were dating some guy from the chess club, and Landon was dating anything in a skirt."

"I guess it started the summer after our sophomore year of college. Landon was back home visiting his parents, and I was on summer break from Mississippi State working three days a week at the pharmacy." Neecie's face took on a faraway expression. "I'd changed a bit since high school."

"College will do that," Bliss said, thinking not of herself but of Bob. "Or maybe it's just life that changes you."

"True." Neecie reached for a praline. "Anyway, I was flattered that Landon even noticed me, what with him being, well, Landon."

Bliss nodded. She of all people understood.

"I can't explain it except to say that we fell head over heels in love in a very short time. It was around then that Bobby's wife died. I tell you, watching that man mourn Karen and try to take care of that baby girl all by himself did something to Landon."

"Oh?" Bliss touched her lips and tried not to think of Bobby with another woman. Silly, but it bothered her even though she knew the story of his brief marriage.

Neecie set the remainder of the praline on her plate.

"Landon changed. I mean, really changed. Two weeks after I went back to Mississippi, he called and said he wanted to marry me as soon as football season was over. You know how Landon is. It's hard to say no to someone so charming." When Bliss nodded, Neecie continued. "He came home for Christmas with a big diamond ring and the key to a two-bedroom apartment, both of them courtesy of the football coach and the alumni association."

"That's very romantic," Bliss said. "But how did your parents feel about this? Kind of sudden, right?"

"Sudden, yes. They wanted us to wait, to spend more time getting to know one another. But hey, we thought we knew better. You know?"

Neecie pushed the praline across the plate, and Bliss rose to grab the dish towel. "You don't have to tell me this."

"I want to," she said. "Anyway, I loaded the car with everything I needed to take back to school and let them think I'd listened to everything they said. I drove out to the old schoolhouse and left my car parked out back by the bayou. Landon picked me up in his Firebird, and we rode all the way to Orange, Texas, with the top down."

"So you eloped."

"Yes, I walked out of the courthouse Mrs. Landon Gallier." She swung her gaze up to meet Bliss's stare. "Marrying someone like Landon, well, it was like I'd been elected prom queen and made cheerleader, all on the same day. Isn't that strange the way my first thought was of high school and how far I'd come since then? In a way, it was like I'd never left high school."

"I'm not sure we ever get past that feeling, honey. Not completely," Bliss said. "What I mean is, those years—"

"Bliss!" Bobby's yell echoed through the shop. "Bliss, where are you? Bliss!"

"Oh, my word. What is wrong with that man? Bobby!

Neecie and I are back here," she called. "We're still in the kitchen. I know you and Landon have probably already been to Iberia and back but—"

Bobby fairly flew into the room, eyes wide and face pale. "Bliss," he said as he seemed to be hanging on to the door frame for support. His mouth moved, but he couldn't seem to say the words. Finally, he managed one: "Wedding." Then another: "Emergency."

Bliss and Neecie exchanged glances. "Amy's wedding?" Neecie asked.

"Is there something wrong with Amy?"

"No," he said. "Not Amy, the wedding." He shook his head. "No, I mean, the news, today. . ."

"Something on the news today related to Amy's wedding?" Bliss asked. "Are you sure?"

Bobby nodded. Then he said another word: "Fire."

fifteen

It took a few minutes, but Bliss finally got the story out of Bobby. The shopping center where Divine Occasions was located had gone up in flames. Once again, Amy Tratelli was without a wedding planner.

And her father was without hope—or at least he looked to be.

"You don't understand, Bliss," he said as he shook his head. "I promised her not an hour ago that I would make this wedding perfect. I promised." He paused. "Like as not, the files were already toast by then."

Bliss exchanged glances with Neecie. "At least she still has her dress, Bobby. Is there any way Amy might consider scaling down the wedding a bit?"

"Scaling it down?" He looked skeptical. "You mean like uninviting people?"

"I guess that wouldn't work," Bliss said.

They sat in silence for a few minutes. Then Neecie grinned. "You know, Bobby, I think I have a solution."

"You do?" Bliss and Bobby said at the same time.

"Sure." Neecie hopped off her stool and began to pace, all signs of her prior distress now gone. "Your daughter's getting married in three weeks, right?" When Bobby nodded, she continued. "Okay, well, you have the church, right?"

"Yes, that I do know. The reverend confirmed last week."

"Okay, and Amy has the dress. I know that for sure. So it's a simple matter of phoning the tux rental shop where the groomsmen were already measured." She swung her gaze to meet Bliss's stare. "Could you do a wedding cake and something for the groom? I'm thinking simple elegance for six hundred."

"Six hundred?"

Neecie nodded. "General rule of thumb in a wedding is that half the people who are invited actually show up. Now, what do you think about a casual chic theme?"

"Neecie, I don't have a clue what that is, but if you think Amy will go for it, I'm in."

"I think she just might. I've got a florist friend who does amazing things with lilies, and there's that beautiful rose arbor in my shop that would look just right decorating the altar at the church. Add a few tulle bows on every other pew, a carpet runner of some sort, and we're in business."

Bob nodded. "All right by me."

"Now, about the reception. Do you have any invitations left? I'd like to see what they say in regard to the reception."

"I've got invitations in the truck, but the reception was supposed to take place in the garden, outside the church. That's already been reserved by another bride."

"Get me an invitation anyway," Neecie said.

"Sure, just a sec." Bobby bounded out of the room with what seemed to be newfound energy.

"Neecie," Bliss said, "have you lost your mind? We can't put on a wedding for six hundred people."

"Sure we can," she said. "Where's your confidence?"

"It took a reality check. And as for baking a—"

The front door slammed, and Bliss winced. "Got it," Bob called.

Neecie accepted the invitation and opened it to read the details. "Okay, well, looks like you're having a crawfish boil out at your place."

"What?" Bobby reached for the invitation. "That's not what this says. This says reception and dinner to follow."

"Exactly." She retrieved the invitation and handed it to

Bliss. "Do you see anywhere on this thing where they've specified a location for the reception?"

Bliss glanced over the writing, then shook her head. "No, I don't. I suppose they'd planned to usher the guests out the church door to the outside garden."

"Then we're having a crawfish boil. This is Louisiana. People will be intrigued. Let me ask you this, Bobby. You know that old Piper airplane of yours?" When he nodded, she continued. "Can you land that thing anywhere near the church?"

"Sure," he said. "There's a field south of the building that would work just fine as long as it's not too wet. Why?"

"Because that's how our bride and groom will be making their exit. It does hold three, doesn't it?"

"It can in a pinch."

"All right, so do you think you can assemble a crew to do a crawfish boil? I'm talking potatoes, corn, the works. And we'll want to have a band. Oh, I know, there's this guy in New Iberia who's really good." Neecie pointed to Bliss. "Paper and pen. This is good, but I know I'll forget half of it if I don't write it down."

Bliss scurried after the paper and pen and returned to find Neecie and Bobby discussing how best to get the guests from the church to Bobby's place. "I've got it," Bliss said. "What if we send them up the bayou by pirogue? Your place is only a mile or so upstream, and it will be such a pretty ride this time of year."

"Pirogue?" Neecie asked. "Do you know how long it would take to move six hundred people by pirogue?"

"I'm just thinking of the wedding party. We can get the rest of them there by limo. I'm sure there are plenty of them available."

"I've got a better idea. A client of mine married into a family that runs airboats up and down the bayou." She paused. "What if I call her?"

"Sure."

She pulled her cell from her pocket and punched in the number. Five minutes later, they had a dozen airboats and their captains to chauffeur the guests to the reception.

It was Bobby's turn to work his magic. He picked up his phone and called the office. "Mrs. Denison, could you get me James at Richards on the Atchafalaya River? Their number is in my. . . Oh, you already have it. Great." He exchanged smiles with Bliss. "Thanks. Yes, please put me through."

In a conversation that seemed to be more about hunting, fishing, and a newborn colt than catering a wedding reception, Bobby negotiated a deal to have an entire Acadian feast provided on the day of the wedding. In exchange, the colt they had chatted about would belong to James.

It was a hard bargain but a fair one, according to Bobby.

"All right, so everything's under control, right?" Neecie said.

Bliss opened her mouth, then shut it tight. There were only two ways she could accomplish the task of baking the cakes in the time frame that Neecie asked. Either she bumped someone else from the schedule, or she broke her own rule of only doing one wedding each week.

"Well, actually," Bliss said, "I'm pretty much booked that week."

Both sets of eyes swung to stare in her direction. Bobby nodded.

"I can't ask that of her," Bobby said. "Everyone in town knows how busy Bliss is."

She was about to agree and thank him for understanding when she tumbled into the depths of his blue eyes and was lost. "No, I can do it," she heard herself respond. "It'll be my gift to your daughter."

The eyes blinked, and their owner rose to cross the distance between them. "You won't be sorry." Bobby's arms gathered her to him, and she rested her head on his chest. Across the kitchen, she caught Neecie looking at them. Was that a tear she saw glistening on her friend's cheek?

Landon. Of course. She'd almost forgotten.

"Bobby," she whispered, "don't forget we've got another problem." She discreetly gestured toward Neecie.

"What can we do?"

"I wish I knew the answer to that," said Bliss.

"Let me think on it, okay?" he replied.

Bob pulled away from the curb and drove his truck toward New Iberia. He'd given up on going to work today. Tomorrow he'd make up for lost time. Today he was too busy making up for lost years.

He pulled into the parking lot of Harrison House a short while later, then knocked on the door. A dour-looking man with a thick patch of gray hair and an uneven set of false teeth answered the door.

"Landon Gallier, please," he said.

"Wait here." The man nodded, then closed the door. Bob waited a full five minutes before reaching to knock again. The same fellow answered the door. "I told you to wait." His eyes narrowed, and he peered down his nose at Bob. "You his probation officer?"

"Pro—? Um, no, I'm his friend."

The old man snorted. "Ain't nobody 'round here got no friends. You the law for sure, and ain't nobody comes to the door for the law. That's probably how you got that nasty bump on your head. Probably got popped 'cause you're the law."

Bob shrugged. "Look, I'm not the law." He pulled a business card out of his pocket and handed it to the man. "Give this to Landon and tell him to call me." The man ignored him until Bob retrieved a twenty from his wallet. "If I hear from Landon Gallier before sundown, you'll get this the next time I see you."

The old fellow looked skeptical. "How am I going to know

if you're pulling my leg?"

"You won't," he said slowly, "but what do you have to lose?"

For some reason, Bob's truck turned left instead of right at the city limits, and he found himself sitting in front of the Cake Bake again. Neecie was back at work inside Wedding Belles; he could see her standing at the counter talking on the phone.

He almost threw the truck into reverse, but something told him he'd be better served to go see Bliss before he headed back to work. When he walked up to the cake shop, he found the door open to the March breeze and Bliss at the cash register ringing up a sale for a retired teacher.

Rather than make his presence known by going inside, Bob hung back on the sidewalk and watched Bliss make conversation with the elderly matron. He'd leave for work in a minute, for no doubt Mrs. Denison was wondering where her boss had gone off to. And there was the pile of work he'd allowed to grow on the corner of his desk.

Still, there was no denying that age had been kind to Bliss. Even back in school when Bliss had no idea how beautiful she was, Bob had known she would never lose her sweet smile and bright eyes, no matter what her age.

She glanced his way and aimed that smile at him, and Bob's heart lurched. "Easy, boy," he whispered as he slipped the guard back over the place in his heart where he kept his love for Bliss. She'd let him kiss her. That had to be enough for now.

Or did it?

"Can I help you with that, Mrs. Boudreaux?" he asked as his former high school English teacher attempted to pick up three cake boxes at once.

"Well, hello there, Robert." Her eyes narrowed, and she stared at him as if he'd forgotten to turn in his homework. "What in the world happened to you? Are you still playing football without a helmet?" She chuckled. "I remember when you nearly knocked Landon Gallier unconscious right on my front lawn."

What she didn't know was that particular time he'd landed a well-placed blow on his best friend to temporarily end Landon's bragging about his possible conquest of Bliss. Far as Bob knew, Landon never thought again about seducing Bliss. For that matter, he never bragged about Bliss's possible crush on him until yesterday, either.

"No, ma'am." He winked at Bliss, then followed Mrs. Boudreaux to her car. The task complete, he loped back inside and grinned as he placed three quarters on the counter.

"My tip," he said.

"You're joking," Bliss responded.

Her laughter was contagious, and soon Bob felt as if he might never stop smiling. But then he'd felt that way since Bliss came storming back into his life.

Or, rather, since the day he got his foot stuck in her door.

"What time do you close?" he asked as he rounded the corner of the counter and joined Bliss beside the register. "I've got this new plane I'd like to take out for a spin, and it wouldn't be the same if I went alone."

"Is that a pickup line, Bobby Tratelli?"

He inched closer and feigned innocence. "If it is, did it work?"

"Maybe. Come back here at four and see," she said.

He checked his watch. "Four it is," he said. "And just so you know, I plan to sweep you off your feet."

"You plan to do what?"

Bob closed the distance between them and gathered Bliss into his arms. "I can't think of anyone I'd rather spend time with, Bliss Denison, and life is too short to keep that important information from you."

She looked up at him, and his heart lurched. "Wow, that must have been some conversation with Landon."

"Forget Landon," he said. "Are you going to let me work

my magic and sweep you off your feet this afternoon or not?" Before she could respond, he continued. "Wait, you don't have to answer. Just kiss me."

Her confused look and the kiss that followed broadened his smile. Bob wore that smile all the way to the office, even when his assistant gasped at his appearance. "I fell while jogging," he said.

She tagged behind him a half step as he shrugged out of his jacket and tossed it onto the coatrack. "Oh my. Have you seen a doctor? That looks absolutely awful."

"I don't need a doctor," he said, "but thank you for your concern."

"Consider it, please," she continued. "You just never know what you'll find when the Lord lets you get hurt like that. Why, if it hadn't happened to Bliss, she would have no idea about that—" Mrs. Denison placed her hand over her mouth and shook her head.

He stopped short and gave her a sideways look. "Bliss would have no idea about what?"

Bliss's mother froze for a second, then recovered. "It's nothing, really," she said. "Now, is there anything pressing you need me to do?"

Bob debated whether to continue this line of questioning. If Bliss had something to hide, surely he wouldn't be the one she hid it from. Not with their combined histories going back to a time when lost teeth were a source of joy and braces were still in the future.

Still, if her mother was willing to spill the beans on some information that might be helpful to know, who was he to keep her from it? A few well-placed questions, and he'd have the woman telling him everything.

Then the phone rang, and she skittered to answer it, shelving any possible conversation for now. "Hold my calls unless it's my daughter, please," he said to Mrs. Denison's back as he brushed past to confront the reality of a desk piled high with items he should have handled last week.

Five minutes later, she arrived in his office with a cup of coffee. "I understand you like it brewed extra strong on Mondays. Now that it's past lunch and you're just getting here, I figured double shots of caffeine are probably in order."

He chuckled. Either his secretary was extremely perceptive, or she'd had a conversation with Yvonne over the weekend.

"Say, I don't want to pry, but what do you intend to do about your daughter's wedding? I'm sure the fire has set things back a bit."

Bob wrapped his fingers around the handle of the mug and inhaled the aroma. "It's all under control."

"It is?" Gray brows shot high. "How so, if you don't mind me asking?"

Bob took a sip of the steaming brew, then set it aside to reach for the first file on the stack. "I don't mind at all, actually. The three of us are handling it." He suppressed a smile at her confusion. "That would be Neecie, Bliss, and me."

sixteen

"Considering all that's happened today, I didn't think you'd show up, Bobby." Bliss turned the OPEN sign to CLOSED, then shut the door. "Are you sure you still want to take me flying?"

"Are you kidding? Nothing improves my day like taking one of the planes up." He paused. "Say, I never asked you how you liked flying. You're not one of those white-knuckle types, are you?"

She shook her head. "Are you kidding? I'm fearless."

After making the short drive out to the airfield, Bliss got a look at the plane Bobby planned on taking her up in. If only she could retract that claim of being fearless. Rather than the sleek jet or deco-styled vintage aircraft she envisioned, the body of the yellow plane was barely larger than her car.

"She's a 1946 Piper J3C Cub," he said proudly. "And not just any J3C."

Bliss tried to keep the quaver from her voice as she replied with a casual, "Oh?"

"That's right. My father bought her from an outfit in Memphis right after he purchased this property here." He lovingly patted the school bus yellow plane. "She was the first in the fleet. I thought we'd lost her once when we couldn't get a radio signal, but some excellent research by my buyer turned her up in a hangar over in Alvin, Texas."

"Is that right?" Bliss swallowed hard. "It must mean a lot to you."

Bobby gave her a strange look. "Well, of course," he said. "The first person Dad put in the passenger seat after he bought this beauty was my mother. Now I've got the plane back, and it's been completely restored." He gave Bliss a look. "I'd be honored if you'd take that ride with me today."

How could she say no?

Bliss took Bobby's hand and smiled. "Thank you," she said. "I think a ride would be lovely."

"No, Bliss," he responded. "You're lovely."

She tore her attention from the plane to her host. "I'm going to be honest," she said. "I've never flown in a plane so small. Would I sound like a fool if I asked if it's safe?"

"Yes, it's safe." Bobby pulled her into an embrace. "I wouldn't think of putting you at risk." He paused. "I know it's been quite a day, what with Landon's surprise return and the fire, but I just want you to know I think the world of you."

Think the world of me? What does that mean?

"Well, Bobby," she said as she looked up into his eyes. "I think the world of you, too."

"Okay." He frowned. "I'm an idiot. That's not what I wanted to say."

Her heart sank. First a compliment, then a retraction?

"What I wanted to say, Bliss, is that I care deeply for you. Very deeply."

"You what?" She felt as if the breath had been knocked out of her. Did she dare hope she hadn't misunderstood?

Bobby nodded. "I can't remember a time when I didn't feel this way about you. I know I'm making a fool of myself, but I don't want to end up like Landon." Bobby paused. "He has so much regret for the time he lost. I don't ever want to have anything to regret about us."

"Us," she said. "I like the sound of that."

"You do?" He laughed. "Now that's something to celebrate." He gestured to the plane. "We don't have to take her up. I've got plenty of planes to choose from. Or we don't have to fly at all. I can always take you back to the Java Hut."

"No," she said, "this one's special. I'd be honored."

"Bliss, I think I love you," he said as he lowered his lips to meet hers.

When the kiss ended, she looked up into his eyes. "I think I love you, too," she said.

"Right now I could fly without a plane—I'm so happy. I'll settle for taking you for a spin in the Piper, though. Right this way, Miss Denison."

Bobby helped her into her seat, then took over the controls. While Bliss smiled to hide the butterflies in her stomach, Bobby brought the engines roaring to life, then turned the little plane toward the runway.

"You sure?" he shouted over the din.

"Yes, I want to fly with you."

He shook his head. "No, I mean are you sure you think you love me?"

It was Bliss's turn to shake her head. "No," she said.

"No?" He let off the throttle and the plane coasted to a stop. "But you said—"

Bliss laughed out loud. "I don't *think* I love you, Bobby. I *do* love you. Now take me flying."

The little plane rolled down the length of the runway before taking a running leap into the air. Before long, Tratelli Aviation and the Latagnier Airstrip were growing smaller and the clouds seemed close enough to touch. By the time he'd circled downtown twice, then brought the plane down for a landing, Bliss realized she loved flying almost as much as she loved Bobby Tratelli.

When the Piper Cub rolled into the hangar, Bobby shut off the engines, then helped Bliss out of the plane. "I think you told me something up there, but I'm not sure I heard you right. Did you say you loved me?"

"Life's too short to miss out on telling someone important things. Isn't that what you said earlier today?"

"I believe I said something like that."

She smiled. "Then kiss me, Bobby, before another minute passes us by."

Before their lips met, however, Bliss passed out cold.

❧

"Don't be so hard on yourself, Bobby," Mrs. Denison said. "You had no idea the excitement of flying combined with the changes in altitude might aggravate Bliss's condition."

"I had no idea she had a condition."

Bob felt as if he'd been strung up on a wire and left to hang there. One minute he held Bliss in his arms, and the next he was calling for an ambulance, then phoning her mother. Now this.

The woman he loved more than life had a condition. Worse, no one would tell him what sort of condition.

"She loves me, you know." He slid Mrs. Denison a sideways look. "I deserve to know."

"Bliss needs to be the one who tells you, Bobby." She shook her head. "I'm sorry. I wish I had a better answer, but this story is not mine to tell."

He rose and began to pace, feeling more and more like a caged animal as the hours ticked by. When a doctor finally appeared, Bobby didn't know whether to punch him or hug him.

"How is she?" Bliss's mother asked.

"She's stable," he said, "but I must tell you; I don't think we're capable of dealing with this here. I'm going to recommend she be held overnight until her specialist can determine a course of action. We may have to transport her, but if we do, I'm going to expect she will be sedated. The least movement and the—"

Bob clenched and unclenched his fists as the pair continued to discuss Bliss's health. Finally, he could stand it no longer. "Can I see her?"

"I'm sorry, family only."

He looked over at Mrs. Denison. "With her dad gone,

you're the one I'd need to clear things with. I'm asking for your daughter's hand in marriage. What do you think, Mrs. Denison?"

"First off, I think the two of you are well past the age where you need to be asking for my blessing, but I certainly do grant it."

He gave the doctor a level stare. "There, now I'm family. Satisfied?"

A few minutes later, a nurse led him down the maze of corridors until he reached Bliss's bedside. She lay sleeping, her face partly hidden by the machines attached to her.

As he walked toward Bliss, an image came to him of another woman lying in another hospital bed. Karen.

Bob swallowed hard. "I can't do this, Bliss," he whispered. Whatever's wrong with you, I can't watch you go through it."

He turned and walked out of the room, past the waiting room, and into the night. Vision blurred, he walked right into Landon. Bob rubbed his eyes. "Sorry."

"How's Bliss?" Landon asked.

Landon held up the card Bob had given the old man. "When I couldn't get you on your cell, I called the office. They told me you were here."

"What did you do, walk?"

"No, I hitched a ride as far as the highway. From there it was a matter of finding a delivery truck heading for the airport."

"You went to a lot of trouble."

He shrugged. "I'd say it was about time I started doing that, don't you think?" Landon looked around. "Were you leaving?"

"Yeah" came out gruffer than he intended.

"So Bliss is going to be all right? That's a relief. I told Neecie I would call her when I knew something."

"You told Neecie? Does that mean you and Neecie have talked since I dropped you off in New Iberia?"

His old friend looked sheepish. "We talked, all right. I'm

going over there tonight. If the kids'll have me, I want to learn how to be their dad again."

"That's great, Landon." Bob raked his hand through his hair and tried to keep his mind on Landon and off Bliss. "Just don't expect too much at first. It was hard on the kids when you. . . They thought you weren't ever coming back."

"I know," he said softly. "I know. I've been asking God to close the door if I'm not supposed to walk through it. I think He wants us to be a family again. I'm humbled for the second chance."

Bob slapped his friend on the back. "Hey, I wish you and Neecie all the happiness. In fact, what if I was to offer a little vacation for you all, courtesy of Tratelli Aviation? I've got a plane heading for Hawaii this time next week. Might as well be carrying people along with the furniture."

"Furniture?"

"I promised Yvonne I'd help her move. It's a long story." He waved away further questioning. "Anyway, if Neecie and the kids want, they can go with you. I'd suggest you be on the plane either way. I've got some connections at the terminal in Oahu if you need work."

Landon seemed to understand Bob's meaning. "I appreciate that." He shook Bob's hand, then walked toward the hospital entrance. He'd almost reached the doors when he stopped. "Hey, Bob."

"Yeah?"

"You never said how Bliss is doing."

"Go see for yourself." With that, Bob strode to his truck, ready to drive out of Bliss's life. He started the engine, pulled out of the lot slowly, and caught sight of Landon storming toward the truck.

Bob veered away from the crazed man, threw the truck into park, then opened the door. "What's wrong with you?"

"What's wrong with *you*?" Landon yanked Bob out of the

truck. "I got ten steps into the lobby when it hit me—"

"Hey, let go of me." Bob shrugged out of Landon's grasp. "What's your problem?"

"I was about to ask you the same thing." His breath was coming hard now, his eyes narrowed. Landon looked ready to pounce at any moment. "You were running, weren't you?"

"Running? I don't know what you're talking about."

"I'm talking about Karen." Landon poked him in the chest with his finger. "Let me guess. You took one look at Bliss and remembered Karen in a hospital bed. That's why you were in such a hurry to get out of here."

Bob didn't bother to deny it. Neither did he bother to defend himself. The truth was the truth, ugly as it might be. Rather, he turned his back and climbed into the truck.

"Go ahead, Bobby. Run if you think that will work. Hey, but a wise man once told me that if you don't learn anything else in life, you need to learn that who you are is who you are no matter who's looking."

The reference to his dad made Bob wince. "What does that have to do with Bliss?"

"I'm going to let you figure that one out on your own. But, hey, remember how you felt today when you saw me standing in Bliss's kitchen? I'm sure you weren't thinking how great it was to see me first thing, were you?" He paused. "No, you were thinking what a creep I was for walking out on someone who loved me." Landon pointed to Bob. "Well, right now, I'm thinking the same thing about you."

Bob got all the way home before he realized he'd left his house keys in the hangar when he traded them for the keys to the Piper. Irritated, he turned the truck toward the office, only to find a light on in Amy's office when he drove past.

Letting himself in, he strode down the hall to find the vice president of Tratelli Aviation sitting calmly at her desk. "Hi, Daddy," she said.

"Oh, honey, you're a sight for sore eyes," he said as he lifted his daughter into an embrace. "I can't believe you're home."

"I'm home," she said slowly, "but I'm not sure you're going to be so happy to see me when I tell you my news."

seventeen

Bliss woke up to a screaming headache and the sound of someone's alarm clock going off. She blinked several times, but the world remained shrouded in fog. Someone who sounded an awful lot like Mama called her name, but Bliss couldn't make her mouth move in response. Finally, she quit trying and slipped into the soft arms of sleep.

The next time she could manage it, Bliss kept her eyes open and focused on seeing around the fog. Blinking helped, so she did it until the clouds cleared. There stood her mother, a smile doing little to conceal the worry creasing her eyes.

Gradually, awareness returned. One hand refused to move, so she leaned forward a bit to stare at the wires and tubes that tethered it to the bed rail.

"Bliss?" This from her mother. "I'm so glad you're awake. Do you know where you are?"

The words traveled toward her as if rolling down a tunnel. She caught each and pieced their meaning together in time to respond with a shake of her head. Bliss paid for that shake a second later with a lightning bolt that skittered down the back of her neck and jolted all the way down to her toes.

"Easy, honey," Mama said. "You've been in surgery. There's going to be some recuperation time."

"Surgery?" With her free hand, she felt for the spot where she expected bandages to be and found them. "Is it gone?"

Mama smiled. "It's all gone. Nothing more to worry about."

"That's not completely true," a distinctly male voice said. "I'd like to think I might give her something to worry about."

She saw her mother's smile broaden. "You have a visitor,

honey, so I'm going to get some coffee."

"Get me some, too," Bliss said, although Mama seemed to think the request funny.

"How about you and I go get our own coffee at the Java Hut as soon as you get out of here?"

"Bobby," she said softly.

He grasped her free hand in his. "It's me," he said.

"I'm sorry," she said. "I should've told you." His face blurred, then her vision cleared again. "They found it after the accident. I was afraid to tell anyone. Only Mama knew."

"You don't have to be afraid anymore, Bliss," he said. "I've spoken to your doctors. You're going to make a full recovery."

Bliss let her heavy eyelids close. "Good," she said as she flirted with the temptation of sleep. Then a thought occurred, and her eyes flew open. "Amy's cake. I need to bake her cake."

"Rest, honey," he said. "It's all under control."

"But the cake."

Bob silenced her with a soft kiss. "The cake," he said softly, "is no longer needed."

"What?"

He nodded. "You were right. Chase wasn't the one."

Bliss shook her head gently. "I'm sorry, Bobby. I'm really, really sorry."

Before he could respond, sleep overtook her.

❧

"Hospital food is the absolute worst." Bliss shifted positions on the sofa and watched Bobby puttering around her tiny upstairs kitchen.

Bobby grinned and toyed with the preposterous apron he'd tied around his middle. "Then you won't have expectations I can't compete with."

"You didn't have to do this, you know."

"I'm doing this because I want to, Bliss, so relax and let me pamper you."

"But I'm perfectly fine. The doctor told me I could resume my normal activities in a few days." She swung her legs over to let her feet touch the hardwood floor. "At least let me—"

Dizziness overtook her, and Bliss covered it with a smile. "Something smells wonderful. What is it?"

"Crawfish pie. Your recipe."

Bliss felt her stomach growl and welcomed the return of her appetite. "How'd you get that?"

"I'll never tell." He gave her a wicked grin.

Bliss chuckled. "Either Mama or Neecie, most likely." She frowned. "Say, have you heard from Neecie?"

Bobby pointed to the coffee table. "You got a postcard. I put it with the mail. I got the same one. Looks like things are moving slow, but steady progress is being made."

"That's great news."

She reached for the stack of mail and retrieved the postcard with the photograph of a map of Hawaii on it. Reading the lines her friend wrote gave Bliss hope the Gallier family might one day be whole again.

"Dinner's almost ready," Bob said as he made his way toward her. "And I've got a surprise for you."

"Oh?"

He nodded just as someone knocked on the back door. "And that would be your surprise now."

Bob trotted over to the door and opened it while Bliss climbed to her feet. A striking woman with dark hair gave Bob a hug, then turned to Bliss.

"Bliss, may I present my daughter, Amy."

"Oh, Amy," she said with a smile. "I'm so glad to finally meet you."

The brunette embraced Bliss, then held her at arm's length. "Daddy's told me so much about you. I certainly hope he has the good sense to marry you before you realize what a pill he is and take off."

"I heard that, Amy."

She glanced over her shoulder at Bobby, and Bliss was struck by how much she resembled her father. "Good," Amy said.

"I think it's a bit early to talk about weddings, don't you think?" Bliss asked.

Amy and her father exchanged glances. "I'd say timing's everything," Amy said.

Two weeks later

"Bliss, are you sure you're up to this?"

"I'm fine, Bobby," she said. "Besides, it's just a walk by the bayou."

"All right, but how about you humor me and take a rest over here?" He pointed to a spot near the banks of the Nouvelle. "Remember this spot?"

Bliss smiled, then kissed her fingertips and pressed them to Bob's forehead. "It's the spot where I tripped you."

"Funny, I remember it as the place where I fell for you." Bob entwined his fingers with hers. "The last place I fell for you. The first will always be Mrs. Benton's third grade classroom."

"Bobby, you're so silly."

He gathered her into an embrace. "No, Bliss, I'm not. I'm serious."

Then he gave her a serious kiss that lasted until the roar of an airplane's engine interrupted them. "Well," Bobby said, "that looks like one of mine."

Sure enough, the plane bore the logo of Tratelli Aviation on the tail. While she watched, the plane went into a dip and a spin, all the while emitting white smoke.

"Is there something wrong with it?" Bliss asked.

Bobby settled her into his embrace. "Hush and watch," he whispered.

Before her eyes, a question appeared in the sky above Bayou

Nouvelle: BLISS, WILL YOU MARRY ME?

He turned to her. "Will you, Bliss? Will you marry me?"

She looked up into the bluest eyes in Louisiana and said yes.

❧

On the first anniversary of the worst day of her life, Bliss Denison walked down the aisle of the little church beside the Bayou Nouvelle and became Bobby Tratelli's wife. The ceremony was small and quiet, with Landon and Neecie Gallier standing up for them as best man and matron of honor.

The reception, however, was quite a different affair. From its location in a hangar at Tratelli Aviation to the catering done by Bobby's friend the restaurateur James Berlin, the event was a celebration to which all of Latagnier was invited. The Broussard sisters loaned their expertise to everything from the decorations to the streamers tied to the wings of the Piper Cub waiting outside for their getaway.

"Are you sure you don't want to take the limo?" Bobby asked his bride. "I have distinct plans on how we will be spending the honeymoon, and an emergency room is *not* part of the agenda."

Bliss winked. "You've got plans? You told me you waited since third grade for this day. Now help me into the plane, and let's get out of here, Mr. Tratelli."

Bob's father came over to offer a bit of last-minute advice to his son, then turned to give Bliss a hug. "Welcome to the family, dear," the spry elder Tratelli said with a wink. "Don't let my son fool you. He's not near as stodgy as he might act."

"Okay, Dad, enough of that."

His mother linked arms with Bliss. "Dear, I cannot tell you how pleased I am that our son has brought you into our family. The Denisons and Tratellis go way back, you know."

"I do," Bliss said.

Amalie Breaux Tratelli smiled. "Well, then, you'll appreciate the fact that we not only share common friendships, but there's also a crib that Bobby's uncle Ernest made for your grandmother Dottie that happens to be in Bobby's attic. It was used for Amy. Perhaps someday it will be used again?"

Bliss felt her cheeks begin to burn. "But I'm afraid forty-plus is well past that age, Mrs. Tratelli."

"Call me Mom." She grinned. "And there are at least two examples I can think of where women believed as you just said, that they were too old to have a child: Abraham's wife and me." She giggled. "For you and my son, I pray a double blessing."

Bobby wrapped his arm around Bliss and nuzzled her cheek. "What say we go put my mother's theory to the test?" he whispered.

"Stop that," she said.

"You don't mean it," he replied with a wicked grin.

"Then let me rephrase," she said as she weakly fended off a kiss. "Stop it for now."

"When shall I resume?" he said as he looked at his watch.

"What time do we land?"

Bobby laughed. "I like how you think, Mrs. Tratelli," he said.

"Same here, Mr. Tratelli." She paused to blow a kiss to her mother. "Now let's get going."

She allowed Bobby to help her into the Cub, then waved as they rolled away from the terminal. A scraping noise caught her attention, and Bliss twisted in her seat to look for the cause.

There, tied to the back of the plane was a pink Barbie bike with white wheels and pink streamers. Unfurling from the back of the bike was an elegantly lettered sign, no doubt created by the Broussard sisters themselves at the behest of no one other than Landon.

It read Just Married.

❧

Nine months and three weeks later, Robert Tratelli III was born. Four minutes after him came little Sarah Rose.

BLISS DENISON'S CRAWFISH PIE

Ingredients:

2 pounds peeled crawfish tails
1 stick margarine
1 can cream of mushroom soup
1 can evaporated milk
1 teaspoon cornstarch (mixed with equal amount of water)
1 tablespoon garlic powder
½ teaspoon white pepper (optional)
1 cup chopped onion
1 cup chopped celery
¼ teaspoon cayenne pepper (optional)
1 unbaked piecrust (top and bottom)

Preheat oven to 350 degrees. Sauté onions and celery in margarine until done. Add soup, milk, and spices. Stir in cornstarch and cook until slightly thickened (about 10 minutes). Mix in crawfish and pour into unbaked piecrust, then add piecrust top, being sure to crimp edges together. Bake until crust is browned, approximately 45–50 minutes. Serves 8.

A Letter To Our Readers

Dear Reader:
In order that we might better contribute to your reading
enjoyment, we would appreciate your taking a few minutes
to respond to the following questions. We welcome your
comments and read each form and letter we receive. When
completed, please return to the following:

Fiction Editor
Heartsong Presents
PO Box 719
Uhrichsville, Ohio 44683

1. Did you enjoy reading *Wedded Bliss* by Kathleen Y'Barbo?
   ❑ Very much! I would like to see more books by this author!
   ❑ Moderately. I would have enjoyed it more if

   _____

   _____

   _____

2. Are you a member of **Heartsong Presents**? ❑ Yes ❑ No
   If no, where did you purchase this book? _____

   _____

3. How would you rate, on a scale from 1 (poor) to 5 (superior),
   the cover design? _____

4. On a scale from 1 (poor) to 10 (superior), please rate the
   following elements.

   ____ Heroine   ____ Plot
   ____ Hero   ____ Inspirational theme
   ____ Setting   ____ Secondary characters

5. These characters were special because? _____

_____

_____

6. How has this book inspired your life? _____

_____

_____

7. What settings would you like to see covered in future **Heartsong Presents** books? _____

_____

_____

8. What are some inspirational themes you would like to see treated in future books? _____

_____

_____

9. Would you be interested in reading other **Heartsong Presents** titles? ❏ Yes ❏ No

10. Please check your age range:

    ❏ Under 18   ❏ 18-24

    ❏ 25-34   ❏ 35-45

    ❏ 46-55   ❏ Over 55

Name _____

Occupation _____

Address _____

City, State, Zip_____

Louisiana BRIDES

3 stories in 1

Devoted to their Louisiana bayou homes, three women find love while being pulled from their Cajun country.

Titles by author Kathleen Y'Barbo include: *Bayou Beginnings*, *Bayou Fever*, and *Bayou Secrets*.

Historical, paperback, 368 pages, 5³⁄₁₆" x 8"

Presents

Great Inspirational Romance at a Great Price!

Heartsong Presents books are inspirational romances in contemporary and historical settings, designed to give you an enjoyable, spirit-lifting reading experience. You can choose wonderfully written titles from some of today's best authors like Andrea Boeshaar, Wanda E. Brunstetter, Yvonne Lehman, Joyce Livingston, and many others.

When ordering quantities less than twelve, above titles are $2.97 each.
Not all titles may be available at time of order.

HEARTSONG
PRESENTS

If you love Christian romance…

$11.⁹⁹

You'll love Heartsong Presents' inspiring and faith-filled romances by today's very best Christian authors. . .DiAnn Mills, Wanda E. Brunstetter, and Yvonne Lehman, to mention a few!

When you join Heartsong Presents, you'll enjoy four brand-new, mass market, 176-page books—two contemporary and two historical—that will build you up in your faith when you discover God's role in every relationship you read about!

Imagine. . .four new romances every four weeks—with men and women like you who long to meet the one God has chosen as the love of their lives…all for the low price of $11.99 postpaid.

To join, simply visit www.heartsong presents.com or complete the coupon below and mail it to the address provided.

Mass Market 176 Pages